P9-CND-589

OTHER BOOKS BY JEFFREY LEWIS

Meritocracy: A Love Story
The Conference of the Birds
Theme Song for an Old Show

ADAM the KING

ADAM the KING

A NOVEL BY

JEFFREY LEWIS

OTHER PRESS · NEW YORK

Production Editor: Robert D. Hack

Text design: Jeremy Diamond
This book was set in 11 pt. Janson Text by Alpha Graphics of Pittsfield, New Hampshire.

10 9 8 7 6 5 4 3 2 1

Printed in the United States of America on acid-free paper. For information write to Other Press LLC, 2 Park Avenue, 24th Floor, New York, NY 10016. Or visit our Web site: www.otherpress.com.

Library of Congress Cataloging-in-Publication Data

Lewis, Jeffrey.
Adam the king : a novel / by Jeffrey Lewis.
p. cm.
ISBN 978-1-59051-284-5 (alk. paper)
1. Jewish men–Fiction. 2. Weddings–Fiction. 3. Middle age–Fiction. 4. Rich people–Fiction. 5. Life change events–Fiction. 6. Summer resorts–Fiction. 7. Maine–Fiction. I. Title.
PS3612.E965A65 2007
813'.6–dc22

2007028084

Publisher's Note: This is a work of fiction. Names, characters, places, and incidents either are the product of the author's imagination or are used fictitiously, and any resemblance to actual persons, living or dead, events, or locales is entirely coincidental.

to Gayle and Sarah

CHAPTER 1

ADAM AND MAISIE HAD THE WEDDING OF THE the year that year in Clement's Cove. And they were no longer young. He was in his fifties and never been married. She'd been married once, for about twenty minutes to a Navajo chief outside Taos and later she adopted two little Chinese girls, but mostly she had lived alone. They invited everybody as if it were once in a lifetime. Their families that hardly knew each other and probably never would, old friends, newer friends, an ecumenical crowd, those who got rich and those who didn't, those who invented something and those who played along, government guys, research guys, investment guys, TV guys, a few artists, a couple writers, doctors and lawyers and wives, ex-hippies who started country businesses and those whose best days were thirty years behind them. The meritocracy in all its multiform display. And they invited everyone in Clement's Cove, too. All the year-rounders, the people who weren't from away. A big tent, as the politicians used to say. And it was a very big tent. They had to clear trees to fit it on the land, a tent of Camelot or the Thousand and One Nights.

The caviar was flown in, the lobsters were rushed from Stonington, the rolls were baked that morning in Paris. Bloch paid for everything, though the Maclarens were still as rich as kings. It was his pleasure to pay. It was his desire. He attended to every detail, the flowers, the chairs, the valet parkers who came from Boston and had to be taught about the outcroppings of glacial ledge in the fields, the linens, the shuttles from the airport, even the weather, he would have fixed the weather if he could, he would have sent planes to seed the sky or do whatever they could do. But the weather report was bad and there was nothing that planes could do. In a way the wedding was an extension of the house that Bloch had built, the kind of place that people in places like Clement's Cove would once have called a folly, to build so outsized for the cove, and in the old shingle style, with a copper roof and a turret from which to see the sea in many directions and a flagpole like the mast of a ship and its porch wrapping around and around as if once you were on it you would never get off it. Bloch's Folly. He had built it all to surprise her. It was as if Maisie were a girl being blindfolded at her birthday party and couldn't take the blindfold off until somebody said "now" and the cake or the present would be there and she could like it or not. When she saw the house for the first time, all that I heard that she said about it was that it would be nice if it had a lap pool.

Maisie didn't care about the details of weddings, though she was happy enough that Bloch did. Somebody had to, so why not? She would be there and that was enough. What Maisie cared about were her two little girls, whether the day would be too much for them and if they would feel a little lost and who would take them for a walk. Whereas Bloch cared about Maisie as if the world boiled down to her. Maisie and her little girls and if he could do this one thing right.

All morning the catering trucks came and went, and the pickup trucks of the workmen, and the FedEx vans from the airport, like a parade in a children's book, the whole realm turning out with its tribute. The morning darkened as it went. The storm was coming from the south. It was the first weekend of September and there were remnants of hurricanes around and Bloch checked the sky and wondered.

I was one of the ushers that day, Cord and Teddy and I, and Maisie's brother and a few Maclarens I hardly knew. I watched the morning go gray and still from my own house across the cove. Most of the summer folk of Clement's Cove were gone but I had stayed on for this. Melissa was out in California packing for Berlin, where I had a fellowship and a book to write. Our own cottage in the cove could have fit into Bloch's garage. Cord's, which had been in his family since the twenties, was twice the size of ours and I had thought that was as it should be. I hadn't wanted to come in and buy a place larger than my old friend's. But Bloch had no such social thermostats to control him. Or perhaps he did but they were not reliable, they were prone to making mistakes, Bloch when he came to the moment of his life when he felt he was going to finally live it didn't know quite what to do. Maisie was his compass. Do it for Maisie. And if she didn't want it? Then back to the drawing board. Bloch was in a sense a purer creature than I. He had made all the money, for one thing. Billions. Bloch had made billions. The thing Americans did, make money, the thing that an American would do if he could. And all the time he had made it, he was storing himself up for the day when he would begin to live.

A tabula rasa, in a way. But if that's what he was, then how did you explain his terrible secret? When he was young, Bloch was the driver when Maisie's sister Sascha died in a crash. This happened when we were all staying at Cord's, just out of college, on a weekend in September when we were sending a friend off to war. How do you wind up close to a woman whose sister you killed in a crash? You are sincere with her as if you were standing naked before God. Or that's what I imagined anyway. Impossible for anyone to fathom. But then the crash had never been about it being Bloch's fault. It had been more about others, like Teddy and Cord and myself, needing someone to blame. And Maisie, who was wise in enough things, could probably see that, just as Harry Nolan, Sascha's husband, the friend we were seeing off to war, had seen it right away. It took many years for me, and even then I wasn't sure. Once in California Bloch saved me my job but I was never very grateful because he had been driving that car. And now he was marrying Maisie. And he had built this rich man's domain, that he could have built anywhere, but built it here, near where Sascha died. And he chose Cord and Teddy and me to stand up for him, who'd blamed him and probably tormented him and been slow to forgive. It was as if all his adult life, every moment he wasn't making money, Bloch had been quietly searching, in the same way other men search for a fountain of youth, for the antidote to tragedy, and now at last he had discovered, in a kind of mirror image of the past, burnished by time, something at least worth putting to the test.

On the coast of Maine the rich don't really believe in cars. They believe in boats more than they believe in cars. But they still have to get from here to there and only a few came by boat on this afternoon of glowering skies. By three o'clock the fields around the cove were spotted with BMWs and Volvos and the pickup trucks of the locals and the taxi shuttles from Bar Harbor airport where the private jets came in. Cord and Teddy still looked good in tails whereas I felt shoveled into mine. There were even rumors, courtesy of Cord, that Teddy had gotten lucky with a bridesmaid the night before. Teddy too old to grin in the old sheepish way when confronted with it, but there it was or there it wasn't. He who still led an anxious, disordered life, had given up writing in favor of a bicycle shop in Connecticut but more recently had careered around the country in one of those quests to screw one last time all your old lovers. If he was melancholy about it, he didn't say so. Cord, by contrast, the retired banker, who made a fortune helping out our classmate Fred Smith at Federal Express, was the first of us to retire to Clement's Cove year round and to lead what seemed the shorthand version of the good life, three great athletic kids who went to the public schools, charities, community involvements, wife out fighting the Wal-Mart coming in. Cord welcomed me to Clement's Cove, and welcomed Bloch in turn, when he bought the largest lot of all at the head of the cove.

Maisie still had her looks that day. She had endured Taos and Navajo tribal politics and gurus and throwing her money away and years alone and a second bout of Hodgkin's and still her red hair flew around in a perpetual tempest. They say red-haired people age less than others and it seemed true enough of Maisie. Her face was chubby, her green eyes still gave you hell on an instant's notice, and in her Vera Wang creation-of-the-day she somehow still looked like a virgin, albeit one who wouldn't last for long. Maisie had gotten used to money again. Bloch had allowed her to get used to it. And she had allowed him to get used to spending it, he who was the one who'd always turned the lights off when people left a room.

They stayed apart from one another before the wedding. A tradition here, a tradition there, pieced together like their lives. Bloch stayed in the house that had hardly been lived in and tilted his bowtie first one way then the other and pushed back his wiry hair so that no one could say he was hiding the receded hairline and rued his bulb of a nose that would not take a vacation for even a day and stared at his cello in live horror. Was he really going to play it? He had promised Maisie. She had made him promise. He had practiced for twelve years and no one had heard him yet.

A tradition here, a tradition there. A rabbi, a minister, each playing a part they were slightly unfamiliar with, polite to a fault, making it up a little as they went along, as if "Judeo-Christian" were a vaudeville act that could work out after all. Maisie's girls angelic with their flowers. The locals as dressed up as anybody else. The tent shuddering in the rising winds. The old aristocrats on the Maclarens' side, tall on average and a little stooped and if they were perplexed by anything, not showing it. Meanwhile we ushers seemed determined to look younger than we were. Cord's hair still seemed golden that day and Teddy's gaunt sunken look pretended to have mischief left and I sucked in my stomach.

And then the rain began. The minister recited Bloch's good deeds. The rabbi noted Maisie's courage. When Bloch kissed her, it was with lips so light they would not leave a mark on air, a phantom kiss, a kiss no one could see, you could see their lips approaching, you could see them almost touch . . . and then it was on to the music and the party and the next day it would be the lead wedding in the *Times*, the one where they show the couple in some happy, candid pose and tell little anecdotes about them to suggest how well they'll get along. In this case, the *Times* reported on the merciless storm that nearly blew down the tent and how the bride's father was among the guests who gripped the tent poles to keep them stable and how the storm began its howling in earnest just as the bridegroom, an amateur cello player, began regaling his guests with Saint-Saëns's "The Swan." The *Times* reported that Bloch played magnificently, undaunted by the storm, with a Nicolaus Kittel bow from 1853 that he had acquired in Budapest for ninety-one thousand dollars. In truth he played a little bit like a madman giving the performance of his life. Rain dripped down on him. Table ornaments flew around in the wind. People huddled under their jackets and in the dry spots and, as the paper reported, held onto the tent poles to keep the whole thing from folding up. And perhaps because Bloch played as if the howling storm were the counterpoint to his soul, no one left.

I didn't return to Clement's Cove for a year and a half. The book, the fellowship, the kids in schools and camps, a place we found for awhile far away where I could write and Melissa could paint. When I came back it was mostly to check up on things. It was early in May in a year when the mud season was slow to leave. Not even the black flies were out. I flew into Logan from Europe and drove directly to Clement's Cove on a bone damp afternoon. The road down to the cove twists back on itself in descent so that through the clearings you can see where you're going before you get there. I strained to see our own little house in its bed of trees and Cord's with its perpetually falling-down dock and several more, of the neighbors, all shuttered and stoic, like faithful servants in an old story waiting in silence for their master's return. I couldn't see Adam and Maisie's house because it was out at the head of the land, but when I turned into my own dirt drive and descended to the choppy gray water, there it was. Or rather, there was the burnt-out hulk of it.

I stopped the car, the way you do things, make certain gestures, just to prove to yourself the world's somehow changed. Adam and Maisie's house, Bloch's Folly, a burnt-out hulk. The walls stood, stained and scarred, but the windows were all broken and the porch roof collapsed and the copper roof was fallen in. It was worse than if it had been reduced to ashes. It was as if it had left a ghost behind.

A car was parked in the circular drive but I couldn't see a person around. I turned my own car around and drove over on the lip of road that hugged the cove. Some makeshift, temporary gates had been left open at a careless angle. I drove up between the poplar trees to the house. Another of Bloch's crazy gestures, because Maisie loved France he'd planted poplar trees, as if they were lining a straight road in the Ile de France, on the crooked coast of Maine. The trees looked young and a little clueless, as if they'd just been planted yesterday.

I parked behind the green Explorer that I'd seen from across the water. The grounds still smelled of smoke and burnt things.

Whoever belonged to the car must have heard me coming. A small man came out with a smile. He had a yellow pad and had been making a list. Hi. How's it going? Not too bad.

"What happened here?" I asked.

"Not really for me to say. All they told me was to sell it."

"Like this? You're selling it like this?"

"As is. Correct. Why, you interested?"

"No. But I know these people."

"You're ahead of me then. They just told me to sell it. Terrible, huh? This was a beautiful place."

"It was."

"Terrible. A real beauty. You know, they imported seven tons of flagstone from Modena, Italy. A real tragedy. Of course, the flagstone's still intact. Can't burn flagstone . . . Well, if you'll excuse me . . ."

He went back inside. He left the door ajar and I could see him in the dark hall beginning to make more notes on his pad.

II

CHAPTER 2

IN THE GENERAL STORE WHEN THEY HEARD that Bloch had bought the head of land out to the Cove, Mac who owned the store said that what he heard was that he'd paid over three million just for the land and there was no way it was worth half that, because if you compared it to what Tim Hutchinson over in Orcutt paid for his, which wasn't that long ago, and Tim's piece had frontage too, four hundred feet of frontage, and he paid only a million for his, nine hundred fifty thousand to be exact, so compare the two, what Tim Hutchinson paid, what this Bloch fella paid, it just showed what some of these crazy people from away would do.

Tom Benson the plumber said Bloch's was a nicer piece, it had views to Camden and a lot of Hutchinson's was mud at low, so you couldn't really compare.

Ralph Audry who operated the transfer station said you could for sure compare three million to one million, and he added that generally speaking the prices were nuts over in Clement's.

Bonnie who was married to Mac and ran the store with him said it didn't matter to these people anyway what things cost, they had as much money as God and so who cared.

How much money *did* he have and who was this fella, Lewis Early who was retired from small engine repair and currently collected bottles and cans for redemption asked, and Mac said what he heard was two billion dollars and it was from dot com, and Carl Henry the lobsterman said he heard it was more like five and it was from owning a TV studio and Tunk Smith whose claim to fame was he was married four times said maybe twelve, he heard twelve and it was from playing the stock market and Bonnie said they were all wrong, this is how stories get blown out of proportion, what she heard was one billion, which was still a lot when you thought about it and it came from all of those things that were mentioned but in addition he invented something like tie-dyed, or not tie-dyed, stone-washed, it was like he invented stone-washed jeans or something and anyway who cared, he had as much money as God.

At about that point Verna Hubbard came in for her coffee. Verna cleaned houses and lived in a trailer over in Clement's on land that her father who was a fisherman had had and his father before him and Lew Early asked her what she'd heard and she asked him "Heard about what?" and he said about the big land deal out there to the Cove and if that property that the fella from away bought went for three million then what would hers be worth now? Verna said her whole property was the size of a three-cent stamp and the only view it had was trees and the propane tank and anyway she wasn't selling.

Yeah but they'll be raising your taxes soon enough, Ralph Audry said, who'd been a selectman and felt he was conversant with such things more than the average citizen was.

Verna said if they tried to do that she'd be over to Town Office the next morning and Burt Cummins would be hearing holy hell from her, but anyway she wasn't selling.

In the general store on the morning following the day when Bloch laid the foundation for his house, Con Stephens who was contractor for the stonework was in, but he wasn't talking. Ralph Audry said he'd seen the owner Mr. Bloch himself on the grounds the other day and he looked like an ordinary guy, kind of a short guy and he didn't wear a tie. Lew Early said what he heard was the guy had an architect up from New York and wherever this Mr. Bloch went, the architect from New York walked right along a half a step behind him, if they'd been any closer they would have been Siamese twins. This Mr. Bloch didn't say a whole helluva lot, but he seemed to know what he wanted.

Mac thought the fella better know what he wanted, if he was spending ten million dollars like that. Carl Henry asked who said it was ten million dollars. Mac said just figure it out for pity's sake, if the land cost three, the house was going to cost at least another six, so that would be right close to ten million dollars, by the time you had overruns and the like.

All these things they said were to get a rise out of Con Stephens, but Con sat there on his stool and drank his coffee and said nothing. Mac asked him how he could even drink that coffee, he was being so close-mouthed, but all Con did was grunt.

The talk turned to who was getting the work over there to the Cove and who was hoping to get work over there and Tom Benson the plumber observed that all the plumbing was coming from France so when it broke who was going to fix it. Tunk Smith, who was also caretaker of several properties in addition to having had four wives, said he had fixtures from France in one of his places and it didn't matter, France or Timbuktu, your basic toilet was your basic toilet.

Then Verna came in with Roy her boyfriend and what Roy heard, he said, was that this guy this Mr. Bloch was Jewish, he was a Jewish fella from New York, which finally got Con to say something, he said it didn't matter to him at all, whether the guy was Jewish or Buddhist or Hindu.

In the general store on the day Maisie came to Clement's Cove to see the house for the first time, Verna, who was herself overweight and wore jeans that didn't hide the situation, said that she'd seen her drive past and walking around the place with Mr. Bloch and she was a redhead who could use to put on a few pounds.

CHAPTER 3

THAT THING ABOUT MAISIE AND THE LAP pool. There was more to it than appeared. In 1997 she had had her second bout with Hodgkin's disease. The chemo knocked her down and her recovery from it was slow. She who'd never believed in food fads or exercise fads or the whole nineties sense of "health" as a daily enterprise to substitute for prayer became a devotee of health food stores and gyms and anything that would give her a better chance. It wasn't that she'd changed her mind, it wasn't that she now believed in any of it, it was just she didn't know what else to do and now she had these little girls. The Hodgkin's had come six months after the little girls.

Bloch was part of that program too. Someone to take care of her, someone to take care of them all. She was harsh with herself when she thought of him that way, but she knew that enough of it was true. She knew, anyway, what he wasn't for her yet, and she doubted he ever would be. She didn't know. She didn't want to guess. He was there and that was enough. And for him, too, she thought. She could see his own needs. She didn't oppose them. In a way, she loved him for them. She felt grateful and lucky that he had needs and that her simply being there had something to do with them. A marriage of equals, then?

The house was part of his proposal. She had spent her childhood summers on the coast and had loved it as children will always love their one safe place, but when her parents divorced, the house on Mount Desert became empty and damp and she didn't want to go there. Clement's Cove was where the Elliots had gone forever and there was a piece for sale that was high and had views down almost to Rockland and she wanted a little pebbly beach for the girls and the Cove had such a beach. And so Bloch bought the land. He told her he bought the land. He showed her the plans, too, but she didn't want to see the house until it was built, she wanted the surprise.

Or really, she wanted Bloch to be able to give her that surprise, she wanted to be able to give him that much, she who hated the fact that otherwise she gave him too little. The day he took her up there, the day she saw it for the first time, the day she said it would be nice if it had a lap pool, was the day that he proposed.

But you have to understand, about the lap pool. Maisie loved the coast, the bay, the cove, but the cold water was hard on her now. Something about the chemo or something about the disease. Or something about just getting older. When she was young she'd swum like crazy in it, off Bartlett's or on Singing Beach, and left all the boys astounded. Fifty degrees, sixty degrees, who cared. The boys did, but not Maisie.

And now she needed to swim, for the exercise, for health, for the chance of it, for her two little girls, and anyway she'd always loved to swim, but if the water wasn't eighty-five degrees she'd shiver and feel faint and swimming more in it wouldn't warm her up.

So the pool was for her health and for her spirit and for those she loved, and when she specified a lap pool it wasn't for fashion's sake, she simply thought a lap pool would be a smaller thing and would fit better on the rocky land and it was all she really needed.

On the day Bloch proposed, he tried to think things through one more time. But which things? He wasn't even sure which things he should be thinking through. Whether she loved him enough or not or in what fashion or what love was or whether he loved her enough or was even capable of it or was his soul cold or if it was cold could it be warmed or what about this house, this ridiculous house he'd built and whether it was ridiculous or absurd or crazy or a folly like the locals used to say or a thing of beauty and comfort as he hoped that Maisie would say and whether it mattered what she would say, of course it would matter but would it be determinative and if so, determinative of what. The calisthenics of an agile mind. The one thing that Bloch had always had. But until he started dating Maisie, he never blinked.

How unfair, how untrue. Of course he blinked. He could remember blinking. But only once in a while. But after Maisie, after they ran into each other on a New York street and he managed to untie his tongue enough and she knew something about him, had read something about him, and so a dinner and then a lunch and then a dinner and then a weekend and there'd never been such a thing in his life before, Bloch blinked more. He'd read enough to know that someone like him was called an isolate by the world, and he was an isolate no more, because the one woman maybe in the world to whom he could explain the sickness of his soul and have it actually mean something, the sister of the woman he'd killed in a crash, he'd run into on a New York street.

Seventy-second Street and Madison, across from the Ralph Lauren. What was either of them doing there? They never said. Maisie was carrying a gym bag. Staying at her mother's old place. Bloch in town on business. This and that. One thing and the other. He who'd dated one starlet once, and been taken to the cleaners pretty good before she ran off with a day player with a drug habit, who'd otherwise never "dated" at all, who'd grown as rich as a tick on a dog in California and begun giving it away because he didn't know what else to do, who was fifty-four years old and an isolate who hardly ever blinked, became, with Maisie, a version of a happy man. Careful, reserved, courteous, undemonstrative, worried, precise, still too often on time for appointments, but no longer melancholy. When he proposed to her, he got down on his knees.

This was on the porch of the house in Clement's Cove and she was sitting on a French wicker chaise looking down the bay, and it was after she said whatever she said about the lap pool. Bloch the undaunted. Bloch the guy who took enough chances, when there was finally something he wanted.

He loved the kids. He moved back east. They made their plans. She got better. He fretted and stayed up nights reading the *New England Journal of Medicine*, so that if she wasn't better, if there were signs, he'd be the first to know. And he, too, began to love it on the coast, for all the reasons that people from away always loved the coast, but also for a few things he was almost afraid to say, even to himself, something about the way the land and sea were so intertwined, like lovers embraced. Their weekends there got longer. They stayed awhile. He began to know who people were in Clement's Cove and the people there began to know him, knew his face anyway, the sound of his voice with its traces of old Pittsburgh flatness, his neat appearance, not quite daring yet to be country, when he came in for his paper.

And Maisie, who was more a natural, who knew the coast, who sailed and gardened and cooked and took her kids around and who'd grown up so rich she'd almost forgotten about it, came and went like someone who belonged there, or as if she didn't care whether she belonged or not.

What she said to him once, what he said to her:

"You're the most awkward, funny, ill-at-ease, quiet, confused, dopey, clueless, smart one I've met yet."

"What does 'one' mean?"

"I don't know. I'm not sure. I'm just trying to say thank you."

CHAPTER 4

WHAT BLOCH THOUGHT ABOUT HIS WEDDING, all in all: that he got through it, that she was his now, that all of this was his now, or hers now, that he was a fool to think such thoughts. That the rolls were good. That the lobster was good. That his playing was atrocious. That no one noticed that his playing was atrocious. That society, or what he'd always imagined society to be, or enough of it, was there, and wasn't that a kick too, and how could that have happened to Adam Bloch from Pittsburgh. That the rain was a gift of the gods. That the rain was really something. That she did not love him.

What Verna Hubbard thought about the wedding, all in all: that it was some to-do. That it was nice, it was the right thing, to invite everyone. That Mac and Bonnie were sure all dolled up. That the call from that lawyer in Bangor the other day, saying he represented Mr. Bloch on a matter and would like to talk to her about it at her earliest convenience, what was that all about? That whatever the musical instrument was that he was playing, Mr. Bloch did a nice job of it, it was beautiful, she liked it. That she didn't really like the idea of this big house going up next to her trailer, but if it had to be somebody, and it had to be, because it was in the nature of progress and how things were going these days, then it might as well be these Bloch people, and why shouldn't they be adopting little Chinese girls, nothing wrong with that, she'd do it herself if she had the money. That the bride could put on a few pounds. That he could have kissed her more. That it didn't matter about the storm, sure it was a storm but what did you expect, don't get married on the coast of Maine, go get married in Pasadena, California, if you don't want a storm. That he was playing a *cello*, of course, a cello, what was she thinking, the cello's the one that's that size, Donny Hendricks in Penobscot played one just like it, in the Baptist church, and Donny wasn't good at it at all, by comparison, when he played it was like a toothache. That whatever this lawyer for Mr. Bloch was calling her about, she'd listen politely, of course. That Roy could have come to the wedding with her, it wouldn't of done him a bit of harm, but that was a whole other story that she didn't want to think about or talk about.

What they thought, all in all, about the wedding in the general store: Bonnie thought it just showed what money could buy. Mac thought the lobsters would've been better if they got them right there in Bucks

Harbor, Bucks Harbor Marine, what'd he go all the way over to Stonington for just for lobster? Ralph Audry thought, along similar lines, if they'd hired Pete Ellison over in Sedgwick for the band, Petey's got a helluva band, much better than these guys, wherever they were from, Petey's been playing at the Reef in Castine and all over, and he's good, wouldn't have been a poor choice at all, to go more local with that.

Lewis Early thought they should have postponed it on account of the weather.

Burt Cummins thought that was ridiculous.

Lewis thought it wasn't ridiculous at all, they postpone ballgames all the time, they could have done it just like a ballgame.

Burt Cummins said ballgames don't have out-of-town guests who just have a weekend to be someplace.

But so you postpone it a few hours, a rain delay, that's all, why not, Lew Early said, people get stuck in old ways of thinking and that's when you get rained on.

Carl Henry thought the bride, contrary to what Verna Hubbard was saying, didn't need to put on a few at all, she had a terrific figure for a gal of her years.

Tunk Smith estimated those years to be between forty-two and forty-five.

Carl Henry heard, *au contraire*, more like fifty-two, which was hard to believe but Bonnie said she could have had some work done, of course, and Lew Early said what kind of work and Bonnie asked what kind of planet Lew had been living on, if he didn't know what "getting work done" meant.

Con Stephens, who was still working for Mr. Bloch on the house, expressed no thoughts at all about the wedding, as he felt, given his contractual arrangements, it would not be seemly.

CHAPTER 5

ON THEIR WEDDING NIGHT ADAM AND MAISIE stayed in the house that he had built. In most of the rooms there were only sticks of furniture, the first pieces to arrive, outposts, like the occasional houses you find in old photographs of American cities, where whole blocks have been laid out with nothing on them except these lonely pioneers. Maisie fed the girls wedding cake for dinner that night and read them the story by Robert McCloskey set in Bucks Harbor about a girl who lost a tooth. Old favorite. Maisie's mother had read her the same story, in a year when that story was new.

They ate their cake in the half-empty kitchen and she read them the story in front of a fire. The living room's fireplace was so vast it looked like it could eat the room, but Maisie and her girls cuddled in front of it, lying on sleeping bags and pillows on the floor, like kittens all together. Maisie built the fire because she was the one, between her and Bloch, who knew how to build fires. She'd never been a girl scout but she'd put in her time outdoors. Bloch watched it all like an old dog of the house beholding its settled world. Not the usual thing with him. Then they all went upstairs.

Their bedroom was the one room of the house that was filled with furniture and things, as if it were a place for them to barricade themselves in, like the "safe rooms" the rich build in New York in case people came to rob or rape. Maisie's idea, to fill up this one room and make it livable right away. Bloch understood, but only in a second-hand way, that the emptiness of the rest could be intimidating. He'd only ever lived in apartments. He expected houses to be intimidating. He was doing all this for them, and the sooner the rest of the furniture arrived, the sooner Maisie picked it out, or somebody picked it out, or they just ordered a carload of it, the better, as far as he was concerned. For himself, he could have lived as a monk.

But didn't he want the world to know what he had done? Wasn't that how palaces and mansions and villas and Maine summer cottages in the old robber baron style got built? Bloch wasn't sure, as he wasn't sure about much, except that he wanted them all to be comfortable, and in this bedroom upstairs, and in the little annex next to it where the girls would sleep for now, and in front of the fireplace downstairs when the rest of the cavernous room was dark, and in the kitchen where you could stand up and eat cake in front of the Sub-Zero's open doors, all seemed comfortable, as if right with the world.

Maisie put the girls to sleep and Adam kissed their foreheads and then Maisie got undressed in the bathroom because she didn't like to get undressed in front of people, she liked walking naked but not getting undressed, it was something sexual and she didn't understand it. Not that she didn't understand about sex. She understood it about as much as anybody. But she had become humble about the parts she didn't understand, because it seemed more truthful to be that way than otherwise. She didn't mind Adam seeing her naked. In a way, there was nothing sexual about it. But getting undressed, she felt invaded and she didn't know why. Something about straddling two worlds, being caught between two worlds. She didn't want even his eyes, or especially his eyes, to invade her; and what Maisie wanted, Adam accepted, though he couldn't help but yearn.

Hers was a body that welcomed freckles. They were like ants on the picnic of her body, and there was something friendly about that too. She came out naked and walked around naked and Bloch looked mostly at her eyes and took his pants off and laid them on a chair because he always laid his pants, folded, on a chair, as though he were visiting a cheap whore, though that had never been Bloch's style. In his underpants, sitting on the edge of the bed, the flesh of his stomach fell over the waistband of the pants, yet Bloch was not a fat man. Nor was Maisie fat, though there wouldn't have been many like Verna who thought she should put on a few. Her shoulders were round, her unsuckled breasts still argued against gravity at least a little bit, her hips were broader than they'd been. A milkmaid's body, or so she thought, when she thought about it at all. Both of them were over fifty years old and they'd seen each other's skin.

She went to the window and put open the curtains and tried to see what she could see, across the cove or down the bay. Bloch shuddered when she did this, as if others could then see her naked. And then what? He didn't know, he couldn't imagine it, any more than he could imagine himself standing naked in a backlit window. It was night. The storm was passed and you could see for miles. But was anybody out there? He wasn't going to change her, she who teased him for his fears and his shyness and may even not have liked him on their account, so he said nothing and kept his shuddering to himself and Maisie cupped her hands to her eyes and pressed her nose to the glass so that she could see better and said, "Louie's watching TV."

"You can see over there?"

"I can see the TV's on. That horrible light."

"What's he watching?"

"I can't see that."

"Can you see him?"

"I can't. The room's dark."

"Can he see you?"

"Would you stop it, please?"

But because he said it, she stayed an extra minute by the window. She couldn't let him get away with that. When she finally came to the bed, he was under the covers with a section of newspaper two days old. She got in on her side as if they'd been married forever and he put the paper down.

"So."

"So . . ."

"It looks like we did it," he said.

"It looks like we did," she said.

"Do you regret it?" he said.

"I don't know yet," she said.

"I don't," he said, and his words felt lonely in his ears, it was as if he could hear them abandoned there.

Bloch wished to reach for her then, to reassure himself. But he didn't, because he had learned that when he reached for her to reassure himself she always turned him down. There must have been something in the reaching, an invisible strain of muscle or spirit, that showed through and warned her. It was impossible to fool her, impossible to be bold when he didn't feel bold, and so instead of reaching for her he said, when the room seemed quiet again, their small talk dispersed in the lighter air that had come in after the storm, "I spoke with Jackman the other day."

"Who's Jackman?"

"The lawyer in Bangor."

"About the pool?"

"He called the Hubbard woman. She hasn't phoned him back."

"Is that really the only way?"

"It's the only practical way. It's the way that makes sense."

"I hate her to have to move."

"Do you?"

"If she doesn't want to."

"If she doesn't want to, then I suppose she won't. But I think she will want to."

"Because of what you'll offer her? Just don't say 'people have their price,' okay? Just don't say that. I'll hate you."

"Well. We'll see."

"I hate money," Maisie said. "That's called ingratitude, right? That's what's called spoiled."

"You're hard on yourself," Bloch said.

"When would it be built?"

"The pool?"

"By spring?"

"I'd hope so. It depends."

For a moment Maisie imagined living in Verna Hubbard's trailer. She imagined cooking smells, cabbage and vinegar. She imagined the floor flexing when you walked on it.

She took the clips out of her hair and lay them on the table next to the bed. She gave her hair a shake and rubbed her scalp a little.

"I don't feel like it tonight. Do you mind?"

"No," Bloch said. He tried to make the word sound solid, rounded, truthful.

And because he didn't like to lie to her, even if it was to keep the peace, even if it was to try to be a bigger man than he was, he told himself it was nearly the truth, because of course he minded, but he felt it was a part of life, for people to not feel like it, for people to mind when the other people didn't feel like it, and for the minding to begin to dissipate, like their words in the lighter air of the evening, when you thought about it that way.

She kissed him and moved away from him and they went to sleep.

Bloch dreamed of how lucky he was.

CHAPTER 6

ON ADAM AND MAISIE'S WEDDING NIGHT, VERNA waited up for Roy. There was nothing on TV as usual Saturday night so she put in a tape of *Sleepless in Seattle* and ate a ninety-nine cent box of mints from the dollar store in Ellsworth. She watched the tape even though she knew the end and she ate the mints even though the chocolate on them didn't taste like chocolate and she wondered what Roy could be doing. He was out with Freddy. He said they had a job but Freddy was always saying he had a job. But on the other hand it was Saturday night and if you had a limo this would be the night to have a job. But what would he need Roy for?

She tried his cellphone but it was never on. That was another thing. She asked him to leave it on and how hard a thing was that? He said it wore the battery down but if somebody said to her to please leave hers on, she'd leave it on, if she didn't automatically anyway, which as it happened she did. Roy had his opinions about things. That was the polite way you could put it. Though along with his opinions also came ideas, Roy had enough ideas to stuff a car trunk, and that part about him she liked. Or anyway when they didn't get too crazy, which sometimes they did, in particular when Freddy was involved. But at least he didn't just sit there. Roy, she felt, had the chance of doing something for himself one day, and that was more than she could say for some others.

Not that there were a lot of others, by way of callers. Roy was about it. So where the fuck was he, Verna wondered irritatedly, then worriedly, then more fondly, until it was twelve-thirty in the morning and the sheriff called to say where he was, which was in their custody, in Ellsworth. They put him on and she was so upset she put her hand over the phone so that it wouldn't make matters worse, Roy hearing her in a disordered state. He said on the phone, in a voice that sounded more intimidated than himself, that the situation over there was all a big mistake and he was going to fix it but in the meantime could she come over and be sure to bring her credit card.

By the time Verna got over to Ellsworth, Freddy's wife Marilyn had bailed out Freddy, so that Roy was alone. The sheriff's station was a place that had fluorescent lights everywhere, which in the middle of the night was especially disconcerting, it made you feel like you were in an experiment where they deprive you of sleep. Verna had been in the station before, but not often, and not for anything that you could call outright criminal on anybody's part. Her dad had been driving drunk once and once Roy was in a bar fight, where it definitely wasn't all his fault, but his big mouth had got him in more trouble than should have been the case. Now a sheriff's deputy brought him out after another deputy ran her credit card through the machine. Two hundred fifty dollars, which would, however, as the deputy explained to her, be eligible for a hundred percent refund unless Mr. Soames failed to appear when and as required. The deputy who brought Roy out didn't hold his arm or anything, Roy came out like a free man. He gave her a look like he wasn't going to say anything while in enemy territory and she oughtn't to either, and they walked out to her car.

Verna drove an older Celica that without the rust spots wouldn't be considered in too bad a shape. They were driving away from the station before either of them said anything. Then Roy said his car was still over in Bar Harbor but they could go get it tomorrow, it didn't have to be tonight. In a way it was unnecessary for him to say that, unless to remind Verna he was being contrite and a reasonable man, since Verna was already driving toward Clement's Cove, not Bar Harbor. Then Roy said, "Thanks for coming out for me," and after that they didn't say anything until they were more than halfway home.

Then he asked her if she wanted to hear what happened, because it was not too bad a story really, now that he was going back over it in his mind, he could laugh about it now. Verna didn't like it if Roy was going to make a joke of it, so she said, with considerable plainness, "Sure. What happened?"

So Roy told her, as follows. Freddy had been putting out some advertising where the cruise liners come in at Bar Harbor, for his limousine services. The people on these cruises, they're on vacation, they've only got a few hours, they want to see a few things, money's no object with them. So even though everybody had a good laugh when Freddy bought the old limo, in fact Freddy knows what he's doing sometimes.

So these two ladies from Cleveland come up to him earlier tonight, and the only thing they want to see is where Francesca Romano the celebrated Food Channel chef lives, on account of the fact that on the cruise ship they'd been telling everybody the fact that Francesca Romano had recently bought a house and now lived over this way, and that was the one thing they were all atwitter about. They offer Freddy two hundred dollars just to take them where Francesca Romano lives. You wouldn't want to say no to that. So they all go, in the limo, over to Pretty Marsh, and these old ladies, they don't give a hang about all the Rockefellers, all they want to see is where the celebrated Food Channel chef lives. And he, Roy, was driving for some reason, though he has no idea where she lives, he was just going where Freddy said to go, turn here, turn there, all they've got over there, on Mount Desert, is a lot of high bushes anyway, you can't see anything, not even in daytime, and this wasn't daytime.

So after about twenty minutes or maybe a half hour Roy turns down this dirt road *per* Freddy's instructions, and it's totally unmarked, the ladies are starting to bother, but that's how these rich and famous people like it, Freddy says, their privacy, all of that, he's starting to sound like the guy who did that TV show about the lifestyles of the rich and famous, if she, Verna, happened to remember that.

Roy himself was beginning to have his doubts, along with the ladies, when up ahead, sure enough, there were lights on. So he drives up into this big circular road and there's this house about the size of what the guy from wherever he was from Mr. Bloch built over by her, and before the ladies could like even gasp and ooh and ah, Roy sees this woman with a housecoat coming out of the back of the house somewhere and running through the woods like a crazy person, like any second she was going to start running naked in the woods or something. And he could see she had a cellphone, she had her arm up to her ear like a cellphone, and that was weird too, and Roy didn't like it because, as Verna knew, crazy people were not exactly his type, but anyway the ladies were still going batshit about the house and how big it was and whether it was in good taste or not, considering that this was the Queen of Italian Cuisine's house, and Freddy was telling him, Roy, to cool it and calm down, because the customers were getting what they paid for and the customers called the shots, which Roy actually of course had to agree with in some sense.

But then, okay, they start to leave, because at the same time Freddy didn't want any trouble. So they were leaving, they were back on the dirt road, and suddenly in his headlights straight ahead Roy could see there were these big branches and logs across the road, it was like a big old beaver dam or something, and this woman in her housecoat, she was just piling things up, as fast as she could. And of course it turns out this was Francesca Romano herself. And there was no way around that roadblock, she was as good at building a roadblock as she was good at cooking up a lasagna. Like Freddy and himself the ladies also couldn't believe she could build that roadblock like that, but they were even more excited to be seeing Ms. Romano in person, and were just getting out of the limo so they could go over and introduce themselves and maybe get her autograph when the sheriff's cruiser pulled up. Francesca Romano had zero interest in meeting these ladies. She just wanted all of them arrested for trespass and some other things.

However the sheriff told her he couldn't arrest the ladies because they were just like the male suspects' captive audience or something and so she drops the charges against them but not against Freddy or himself. He and Freddy tried to explain how they just got lost and didn't know where they were but one of the ladies, real helpful, said they were all out looking for Francesca Romano's home but of course she and her friend didn't know it was illegal or anything because they just thought they'd drive by on the road, which was public of course. Jesus. So that was about it. The sheriff took Freddy and himself over to Ellsworth and impounded the limo and then he called her, but now that he's thinking about it, it's almost funny.

That Francesca Romano, that was the part that was almost funny, seeing her running around in her housecoat. And that roadblock she built. Just like a beaver dam.

Verna listened to this whole story but didn't laugh at the funny parts the way Roy did. She laughed a little, but not too much, and when he was done the first thing she asked him was, "So how old were these ladies?"

"Ah, who knows. I mean, they weren't *old* old."

"Thirties?"

"Maybe. Who knows."

"Twenties?"

"Definitely not. Not twenties, for sure. Definitely."

"And they read Freddy's advertising, that's how they hired Freddy? Like, he's got brochures?"

"I guess so. Sure. Why not?"

"Because last time I saw Freddy, he was talking about doing up some brochures but he said no way did he have the money for it yet, he was talking all this stuff about cost-effective, whether it was cost-effective, he'd have to see."

"Well I don't know if he printed something up exactly yet. Hey, who cares, right? He got the customers."

"Yeah. How? And how come he needed you along?"

"What are you saying here, Verna? What are you suggesting?"

"Oh nothin', Roy. Nothin' at all. I'm not suggesting you two shitbags just picked up these girls off the cruise and were just driving them around in Freddy's shitbag limo trying to impress their pants off 'em. And this thing, you think I believe this stupid shit, this fucking story like I'm a moron, two "ladies," *ladies*, hire a limo after it's dark to go look for houses? And then I come bail you out? You call *me* to bail you out? Why didn't you call those whores from the cruise line, why didn't they bail you out?"

"This is a lie," Roy said. "You're getting yourself crazy for a lie."

"Am I?"

"Absolutely."

"Asshole. Dickhead."

By then they were pretty much back to Clement's Cove. Verna blamed herself more than she blamed Roy. When she got home she threw out what was left of the ninety-nine cent mints. She imagined the whores from the cruise ship were skinny.

Roy had to admire one thing about Verna, her capacity to figure certain things out. But he didn't tell her this. He promised to repay her the money. She said he didn't have to repay her the money, he just had to make his court appearances, and he'd need his money for a lawyer, so thank you very much and good-night. The last thing Roy told her was that he was going to fix this whole thing because it was a big mistake, so she shouldn't worry about that part of it.

Roy didn't go to sleep right away because Verna didn't want him in her bed, and while he was up he saw by the phone Verna's note to herself to call Mr. Bloch's lawyer in Bangor. As soon as he saw the note, Roy thought to himself maybe Mr. Bloch wanted to buy Verna out. Why wouldn't he? Her trailer was an eyesore. Even Roy could see that. Roy read the note again with considerable excitement. It made him remember that Verna was sitting on a gold mine.

CHAPTER 7

THE PROBLEM WAS THE LEDGE. ALMOST ALL of the head of land that Bloch had bought was ledge. There was dirt on it and things grew on it but the dirt was thin and the things that grew on it had shallow roots and even the trees that grew for thirty years could blow over in the winter storms. It was a beautiful piece of land but it was fragile and obdurate at once.

Verna's father Everett had kept the softest piece for himself. He had sold off most of the rest in the fifties and then again in the sixties, but Dottie had wanted to keep her garden, which had peonies and unheard-of good tomatoes, and so he moved the trailer over close to her garden, which was on the one deep pocket of soil that was there. The land that was left for Bloch to acquire would need blasting out the ledge with dynamite if you even wanted to put a lap pool in, and you couldn't blast too close to the shore because there were the state laws against it, and in the spine of the land were the high trees that gave it its privacy and majesty so that the architect said for God's sake don't blast there, and if you put in a lap pool too close to the house, so you could see it from the house, the house would become like a California house, modern and convenient, which was the last thing you wanted on the coast of Maine. The lap pool would have to be hidden in the woods but there was no place to hide it in the woods.

And then there was Verna's land. Everett Hubbard had never owned the entire head of land, but if you went back in the deeds you would find more than a hundred years ago or even before the Civil War that the Hubbards and the Masons and the Clements held it all. They were mostly fishermen and the land wasn't good to farm and over time all three families sold off here a piece and there a piece, and by nineteen hundred the rest of the cove with its pretty views and safe water was being sold to the rusticators from Bangor or Boston or even farther away, but Everett Hubbard's father, William, became a kind of a holdout when even the other Hubbards sold, and Everett took after his father, selling when he felt he had to but never all of it.

And now Verna had the little piece where Dottie's garden had been and where Verna still grew a few tomatoes herself and where you could put in a lap pool or anything else if you wanted to because the ground was good for it and it was far enough away from where Bloch had built so as not to be seen. It was on the road coming into Bloch's place, but you could screen that off with trees.

What Bloch thought about all of this was that if she didn't want to sell, she wouldn't sell. It was as simple as that, really. He wasn't going to intimidate her, he wasn't going to scare her off her land, or build high fences around her land so that she'd be living in a prison, or anything else. If she didn't want to sell, she wouldn't, and then he'd think what to do next.

And in fact intimidating her was the opposite of what he wanted. What he wanted was to be accepted here, and he knew the locals were part of that. He wanted to go into the general store and buy his paper and have the people there say hello. After the anomie of California, after the rough and tumble of the various business worlds where he'd made his exceptional pile, after a life lived alone, he wanted finally to live somewhere. He wanted Maisie, he wanted her little girls, to live somewhere too. And of course there was New York, they would live in New York, they would do all the things you do or can do in New York, but he still wondered if New York was somewhere. "Somewhere" meaning that if you came back to a place half a lifetime later, what you remembered, or enough of it, would still be there. Or if the place itself remembered, if the place remembered you.

Bloch remembered more than enough of Clement's Cove. It had never left him, and it was far from happy what he could not forget, but he knew of no other place where he and Maisie had a chance. And she needed to swim and the sea water was too cold and so he hoped that whatever he offered to buy out Verna Hubbard, it would be enough so that she would want to sell.

So he offered her a half million dollars and in addition to move her trailer to wherever she wanted it moved to. He'd come to this figure after talking it over with Jackman, the lawyer in Bangor. Jackman said it was twice what that little landlocked postage stamp of land was really worth. Bloch wanted to offer her enough to be generous and to be seen by her to be generous but not so much that he'd seem like a fool, or someone who was coming in and throwing his weight around, or someone who was disrupting the way life was. He was already dimly, vaguely aware of what some people were saying about his house. When the house was about halfway done he'd overheard workmen talking at lunch and it had frightened him and almost discouraged him. He wanted Verna to be happy and not be mad at him and to tell others what a reasonable man he was.

What he would never say is Maisie made him do it. Or that he was doing it for her or her health or that it had anything really to do with her at all. It was always "we" who wished to acquire Miss Hubbard's land if we could, we who wanted a lap pool. And wasn't it so? He wanted to make her happy. Only to our old friend Cord would he even mention Maisie's name in connection with any of it.

Verna turned down Bloch's offer of half a million dollars. She called up Jackman the lawyer in the days following the wedding and Jackman explained what Bloch was proposing and conveyed the offer and Verna fussed inside herself at first because she'd never heard half a million dollars connected to her name in her life before and didn't know who to talk to about it. All she knew was that she didn't want to talk to Roy. She wanted to talk to somebody who wouldn't be overwhelmed by hearing a half a million dollars and who wouldn't have a prejudice, or something they were trying to get out of it for themselves.

Finally she decided she would ask Cord Elliot, Mr. Cord Elliot, because he was around for a couple of weeks now instead of traveling someplace all over the world like he usually did in September and because she cleaned house for Mrs. Denny Elliot once a week and because Verna's father in his retirement after he was done with fishing had been the prior generation Elliots' caretaker for a number of years and Everett always said all the Elliots were pretty good but this young one, this Cord fella, was particularly pretty good, which had been Verna's experience subsequently.

She knew that Cord Elliot was friendly with Mr. Bloch but not too much more about it than that. It was a chance but anyway she took it. After her half-day cleaning over there she sought him out in his study and told him about Mr. Bloch's offer and asked him what he thought and whether it was a good offer and what should she do.

Cord first had a good laugh because Mr. Bloch had apparently not said anything to him about it and he thought, he said, that it was a little cagey of old Mr. Bloch and wasn't he becoming the land baron of Clement's Cove. Verna said she figured he was. Then Cord asked Verna what it was she wanted to do, what was her gut instinct, as the people in business were always saying these days, and Verna said it was all so sudden, she didn't have any gut instinct, she could hardly think about it but a half a million dollars was quite a lot of money.

Cord asked her if she needed the money.

Verna, who tended to be understated about money because she felt that if she was understated people would believe she was more familiar with it than she was, said she didn't exactly need it but it couldn't do too much harm, that was one thing for sure. Verna said she didn't know what her father would have done. All the Hubbards had always fished out of Clement's and she still had her father's old boat out in the falling-down lean-to she called her "boathouse" and she didn't know about that either.

Cord said it sounded like she wasn't ready to make up her mind yet but if she said no he was fairly sure Mr. Bloch would come and offer her more money than half a million dollars and maybe that would help her decide. Verna couldn't believe at first that Mr. Bloch would offer her more money but Cord Elliot laughed and said again he was fairly sure of it and so she told Jackman the lawyer, politely, no, she wasn't going to sell.

Bloch raised his offer to three quarters of a million and she said no and then he raised it to a million and she still said no. In the meantime she'd been thinking about her father's old boat in its lean-to and how Everett sold off bits and pieces but never sold off all and how she liked the little bit of woods her trailer sat in and the way her tomatoes grew strongly like her mother's had. And who knew what the whole place would be worth in another hundred years?

Bloch made his final offer at a million and a half dollars. Jackman told her it was his last and final offer. The way Bloch thought about it, he could offer her any amount of money but if she wouldn't take a million and a half, which was already so many times more than the property was worth, then she didn't want to sell at all.

Verna thought about all the money so hard that for two nights she couldn't sleep and Roy wondered what was the matter with her. She visited Everett's boat, which he'd built himself in his last years, she sat in the lean-to with it as if asking her father's advice. It was a sleek little boat with a lapstrake construction and less of a prow than the ordinary lobster boat and Everett always said it was going to be his boat for pleasure, not for work, but he died before he ever got pleasure from it. Or that wasn't so. He had the pleasure of building it, the pleasure of coming out to look at it on winter nights, away from everybody else, sitting out there with a charcoal brazier and what he dreamed about. Verna remembered that, or some version of that. But he only put it in the water once, to test it out, and it didn't sink, and that was in autumn, and that winter he died. And she'd never put the boat in herself, she was afraid of it or too in awe of it. Verna didn't even like boats, but she had reverence for this one. She decided it was telling her it didn't want to be moved.

So she said no again, to one and a half million dollars, and Bloch and Jackman made one last try, despite the previous offer being Bloch's last and final offer, Jackman said Bloch would in addition pay for a new plot of land to put her trailer on, but it didn't change her mind.

The next time Adam ran into Cord, on the road going around the cove, he said nothing about his negotiations with Verna Hubbard. They talked about the dolphins that had been coming into the cove recently and the weather and the Republicans and whatever and when they'd talked those through, a bit laconically, because Bloch was still not a big talker even with a friend, Cord decided to ask him about Verna and her piece of land. It was partially, but not entirely, a case of his instinct to tease someone who in his view could use a little teasing getting the better of his instinct for discretion.

"So I heard you've been expanding your real estate empire over there on the head."

"How'd you hear?"

"Confidential sources."

"Actually, she turned me down."

"Smart woman."

"You think?"

"What'd you offer her, a million?"

"More. More than that."

"I'm gonna sic Denny on you pretty soon. After she's through fighting off Wal-Mart."

"Maisie wants this pool," Bloch said.

"What? What kind of pool? A swimming pool?"

"Just a lap pool."

"She wants a swimming pool on the head? She wants a lap pool in Clement's Cove? I've got to talk to that girl. She better go back where she came from. Mount Desert Island, maybe they've got lap pools. Not in Clement's Cove."

"It's for her health," Bloch said. "She can't swim in cold water anymore. She's got to swim to build herself up."

"Can't you put it on your own land?"

"Not easily."

"Well can I tell you something, confidentially? You ought to try to put it on your own land."

"If I could . . ."

"So figure it out. Get that smarty-pants New York architect to figure it out."

"Why do you say that?"

"Don't go getting your undies in a bunch. Listen, Adam, it's none of my business, alright? But you offer someone like Verna Hubbard something crazy, what if she takes it finally? She's going to hate you for it. Sooner or later, one way or the other. And that gets around. That's all."

"You want her to stay."

"She's been here a long time."

What Bloch almost forgot while they spoke was that he'd already decided to give up on Verna and her land. But Cord's suggesting it to him made him wary. He felt criticized. He felt Cord, his friend, was telling him not to be gauche and pushy and to mind his manners. Cord with his plantation noblesse oblige, Bloch thought.

Then he rued even thinking it, because if he couldn't listen to Cord, who could he listen to?

"Or why doesn't she go somewhere where there's a pool, if she's got to swim," Cord went on, about Maisie again. "They've got a pool over in Castine. The Maritime Academy's got a pool."

"Isn't that a long drive?" Bloch said.

But what he really wanted to say, he hesitated to say. Until he said it anyway, because if Cord was really his friend, Bloch felt he should be able to say to him such things. "You want to know? This whole thing confuses me. People buy and sell things all the time. And that includes land. People have been moving from one place to another for the whole history of this country. A willing buyer, a willing seller. It's always been that way. So what am I doing wrong?"

"I'm not saying you're doing anything wrong. I'm just giving you my advice."

"That makes no sense, what you just said. You're only giving me advice because you think I'm doing something wrong."

"Suit yourself then."

"Anyway," Bloch said, "I already decided. I'm not pursuing that anymore. I'm not making any more offers to Verna Hubbard."

"So what were you being so stubborn about?"

"I don't know," Bloch said.

"You want me to talk to Maisie?"

Bloch shook his head that he didn't.

They'd been walking a few steps at a time, walking and stopping and looking around, the whole time they were talking, until they were at the top of the road where it sprung out of the woods for maybe twenty yards before the houses started again and it went down on the other side. It was a pretty little cove that lay out below them, with gray water and a little mud now that it was low tide and there were various docks that were in various states of disrepair, but no boats because it was October and they'd all been pulled. You could see across to various islands and over to Islesboro and Camden and farther down the bay and both men experienced versions of the thought that this was no place to be arguing.

But Bloch's version was darker. Cord thought, rather simply, though not too simply, that the manifest bounty of nature ought to be a reminder for men who were part of it to get along. Bloch still wondered, as he returned to his house down his road with his poplar trees past Verna Hubbard's trailer, if he was really a part of nature's bounty.

Of course he was, of course he was, but on the other hand what if he wasn't? Who decided such things or could you just think it through? Did Cord think such things? Bloch didn't even know. All he knew was that Cord didn't think and Bloch didn't think, neither of them thought, that Bloch should keep trying to buy Verna Hubbard out. And why was that?

CHAPTER 8

After she refused Bloch's last and final offer, Verna tried to keep to herself what she had done. She figured she didn't need other people's opinions about it and she didn't want their admiration either. She didn't think she could stand the embarrassment if she walked into Mac and Debbie's and people started treating her like some crazy hero, like she was nuts but you had to admire it, that she said no to the billionaire from away. And, as well, if other people knew, then Roy would know. You couldn't tell Bonnie, for instance, and not have Roy find out.

So for days she felt giddy with her secret that she had no one to tell, and while she scrubbed other people's floors and brushed their toilets she thought of the million and a half dollars she'd turned down almost as if the money were actually hers, as if the very act of turning it down somehow made it so, or gave her bragging rights over it, anyway. To Verna, turning it down felt almost as good as she imagined having it would feel. Especially if you took in account all the people you could read about every day of the week or saw on television, for whom money that came to them out of the blue only caused trouble. Like lottery winners. Take lottery winners, for a perfect example. You always read about lottery winners where the guy says he's going to quit work, but then what has he got to do all day long, or then there's a family fight and divorce. Verna felt for a couple of weeks as if she had the best of all worlds, but then Roy found out her secret.

Apparently the lawyer Jackman had been out on the Bloch property at a time when workmen were still around and one of Con Stephens's boys overheard Jackman mention some figures and intentions and "the recalcitrance of the owner" on his cellphone back to his office and this percolated among the other workmen for awhile until Tom Benson put two and two together when he observed Mr. Bloch's architect from New York nosing around Verna's trailer one day. The various angles of this story made it to the general store and from there it was inevitable that Roy would learn of it.

In the general store they didn't have the details just right, but it was close enough, and when Roy heard it, it felt like he'd been shot out of the sky, because for weeks he'd been dreaming about that note that was by Verna's phone that said for her to call Mr. Bloch's lawyer in Bangor. His first thought when he heard Mac talking about Verna cold-shouldering the lawyer was that it couldn't be her final decision yet, if she hadn't mentioned any of it to him even once, and so there had to be a way to change her mind, if he could just not get all crazy and mad at her and cause a scene that would make her more resolute than she already was.

Roy's second thought was that this was just like Verna. She hadn't told him because she didn't want him to know and didn't trust him, and why was that? Roy thought he knew why that was. Because she was a bitch and a beast and a moron who had no appreciation of him or the ways he was good to her and protected her, that's why that was. Although Roy struggled to remind himself that this was no way to be approaching it. If he approached Verna with negativity, that was a sure way to fail. Instead he tried to imagine her as some kind of princess, with a crown made of two million dollars kind of lopsided on top of her head, like the crown of a carnival queen. Two million dollars was the figure that had made it to the general store. Somebody had been rounding up.

Roy didn't say anything to Verna right away. Nor did he even show much reaction when he heard it from Mac in the general store, he just nodded as if of course he knew all of that already and had only been keeping tight-lipped in accordance with Verna's wishes. Roy felt he would look like a real ding-a-ling if he was just about the last one to hear about Verna's fortune and Verna's no. But in fact that was the case, mostly because he didn't go in the store much, he spent most of his workdays off somewhere else, with Freddy, for instance, who wasn't from around this peninsula at all, who was from over on Mount Desert and a graduate of M.D.I. high school.

When he was with Verna for the next couple days, Roy acted like a guy with his pregnant girl. It was as if she were pregnant with gold. Verna noticed the difference, but while Roy was still figuring out what he'd say to her and how to lay the groundwork, Verna herself discovered that Bonnie and Mac knew her secret and that everybody in the general store knew it, they'd all been talking about it behind her back for days, and if she hadn't complained about the cost of the chocolate milk going up ten cents, so as to elicit from Mac one of his patented little remarks, concerning how she sure should be able to afford an extra dime these days, she'd still be in the dark.

So if they all knew, then Roy surely knew and was being cagey. Verna, like Roy, felt she had to take care now. After all, she had kept something from him. Something big, in a way, something that was all she could think about sometimes and that she thought about even more because she had kept it from him. That night, the way she decided to phrase it, being a bit cagey herself, or trying to be though she wasn't much for it, she said, "First of all, it wasn't two million dollars."

Roy was helping her with the dishes at just that moment and feeling fairly good about himself for pitching in. He wasn't prepared. He was still, as it were, laying his foundations. For a moment, when she said it, he even had hopes that if it wasn't two million, it might be even more. Though the way she said it, kind of critical-sounding of whoever mentioned that number in the first place, he would have to admit it wasn't likely. "How much are they offering then?" he asked.

"They're not offering anything. It's over," she said.

"It's not over till it's over. You know who said that?"

"It's over."

"So okay, it's over. So just for historical purposes, maybe you could fill me in as to exactly . . ."

"He offered one and a half million and to move the trailer to someplace else, which he'd also buy for me."

"So that's *almost* two million."

"It's not," Verna said. She'd thought about it a lot, and the last thing she wanted was people blowing things out of proportion.

Roy put the dishrag down, though Verna continued to wash. "Why'd you say no, Verna?"

She shrugged and made an extra effort to get the black off the bottom of the pot. Nor did she look at him.

"Why, Verna?"

"Things you wouldn't understand, Roy."

"I know I'm a dummy, I know I didn't go too much to school, but I understand two million dollars, Verna."

"It wasn't two million."

"It was damn close."

"Roy, keep your voice down when you talk to me."

"I was not yelling. I wasn't."

"You were. You were starting."

"Could we have a discussion about this?"

"What do you want to know?"

"If this is absolutely final, for one thing."

"It's how I want to do it."

"But is it final?"

"I don't know. Yeah. No. It's final."

"Well that's piss poor, you know that?"

"Roy, it's not your property. So when do you even get a vote?"

"I get to express an opinion, don't I? It's a piss poor decision, in my opinion."

"Thank you very much."

She scrubbed the bottom of the pot more obsessively, as if the black spot on it was the stubbornness of Roy's mind that she was trying to scrub clean.

"Verna, I'm thinking of your situation, that's all."

"Are you really?"

"Of course I am. Just let's, could we just think this through a second here?"

"Okay, Roy, be my guest."

"What's the property really worth?"

"I never asked."

"Well, what's the most anyone ever offered you before?"

"I don't know. Two hundred thousand, I think."

"That's my point! You got a place worth two hundred thousand!"

"It could be more now."

"Yeah, it could be more now, but basically two hundred thousand, and this guy's offering you, okay, not two, okay Verna, not two million. See, I'm not a bully, I'm not exaggerating. One million seven hundred thousand, including if he buys you another place. That's profit! You could have a nice farm over on the river, you wouldn't have to live in this shitbox if you didn't want to . . ."

"It's not a shitbox . . ."

"For argument's sake, that's all, I'm just saying, no it's not a shitbox, Verna, it's not a shitbox, okay, but if you move you'd have all that money, you put that just in the bank making interest, that interest is more than you ever saw in your thirty-seven years of your life."

"So somebody else'll offer it. If I need the money."

"Nobody else is going to offer it! This is a special situation, it's special circumstances!"

"Would you keep your voice down?"

"I'm trying to get you to listen, Verna! This is your chance of a lifetime!"

"*Your* chance of a lifetime, maybe."

"You know, this is low. This is truly low."

"If I take that money, you going to marry me then, Roy? Have I got to bribe you to get you to be serious?"

"I'm talking about *you*, Verna."

"Yeah well I'm talking about us."

"We talked about all that."

"So okay, and now we've talked about all this. Now can we just change the subject?"

"Just tell me why."

"Why what?"

"Why what? Why what?!"

"Roy, they're going to hear you down the road, you keep yelling like that."

"Don't tell me to keep yelling, Verna, that's just changing the subject."

"I'm not telling you to keep yelling, I'm telling you to *quit* yelling."

"Just tell me why you fucking did this fucking stupidest thing of your life!"

"Because of my daddy, okay? Because he wouldn't want me to."

"Your daddy's dead."

"I knew what he'd be thinking."

"You think he wouldn't want you to be taking care of yourself?"

"This is the last piece, Roy!"

"You buy a farm on the river, you get a hundred acres, you start over, selling off this, selling off that, a hundred years you'll be down to nothing again."

"What's that supposed to mean?"

"This is how the big boys do it."

"The 'big boys.' What do you know about the 'big boys,' Roy?"

"Is that sarcastic? You being sarcastic with me, you bitch?"

"Well don't start trying to bully me then."

"I am, I *was*, trying to look out for you. Your daddy? Your daddy talk to you or something?"

"He did, in a way."

"This is too much."

"I was in with the boat and . . ."

"He talks from boats, does he, Everett does?"

"See, this is why I wouldn't tell you anything. Because you wouldn't understand."

"Fuck me. Fuck me, fuck me, fuck me."

"Oh shut up."

"Did you tell your daddy how much you were being offered? Old Everett would shit his pants, I bet."

"Don't talk about him like that."

"Did you?"

"Did I what?"

"Tell him how much."

Roy threw the dishrag across the room then and stomped around, so that, just as Maisie imagined, the floor of the trailer flexed and echoed.

When he was done pacing the narrow kitchen, he said he was going out.

"Don't be mad at me, Roy," Verna said.

But he left anyway.

He went out to his truck where he kept a pint of vodka because Verna didn't want him drinking in her house and he drank enough of it and listened to CDs and tried to remember exactly how things went wrong here. He'd been caught unawares, he didn't have his proper foundations built, he lost his cool, and so you could blame it on that, but on the other hand you couldn't talk to Verna. Stubborn as a mule, just like she looked like, when you got right down to it. She hid from him, she lied to him, she had this thing about her daddy, and plus it was absolutely true how she looked if she didn't take extra efforts to fix herself up, she looked like a mule or a moron half the time, so what was he doing with her finally, Roy asked himself, he finally had to ask himself this question, of whether he couldn't do better than Verna.

When he asked himself this question was when he got really mad, for all the time he'd wasted and the frustration of trying to talk to that person and be patient with her and be nice to her and what did it all get him, she says she's turning down two million dollars because her daddy who's dead told her to.

When he was drunk enough Roy went over to the lean-to thinking he'd have a little talk himself with the old man. The boat sat in its frame like it was some kind of throne it was sitting on, like it didn't have to talk to a peon at all. It pissed Roy off, he felt stupid and humiliated and like Verna had gotten the best of him and made a fool of him talking about how old Everett talks to her out of boats, and as if to right the situation or at least to quell it, to eliminate it from being a matter of concern, because sometimes you had to admit that the people you counted on were shit and fucked and morons, he gave the boat sitting on its frame a good shove. It didn't move. All he did was leave his handprints on the bright scarlet paint of the hull. The obstinacy of the boat, just like Verna, or whatever, pissed him off further, so he shoved it harder and when it didn't budge then, he yanked at the cradles and kicked them and yanked them some more until one came out and the boat fell forward on its prow like a dead man, and then from Everett's old tools he grabbed an ax to swing at the hull that had fallen. He managed to crack several planks and put ax holes in the foredeck and would have destroyed it all if Verna hadn't heard the clatter and seen the light on. She came over fearing the worst. She cried for him to stop and pulled at his arms and almost got axed herself yet she managed to pull him down and wrestle him and plead with him and finally he dropped the ax as if he had no idea how it got in his hands in the first place. Among other things he was disgusted and had had enough. He got out of her embrace, stood up and dusted himself off, and without another word he left.

CHAPTER 9

THERE WAS NO REAL CONSENSUS IN THE general store about any of this, except the boat part. Everyone agreed that Roy should not have harmed old Everett Hubbard's boat. Whether it could even be fixed or not was an open question. Tom Benson had seen it because he was out delivering propane to Verna and it looked to him like you could lay in a few new planks and get something to match up on the deck and maybe you'd be there, but he was the first to say he knew little about boats and probably it was more complicated than that. Several others put in, though they hadn't seen it, that just from what Tom was saying it had to be more complicated than that.

As for Roy, he was lying low. He hadn't been in the store at all. Burt Cummins said he was over in Bar Harbor, doing who knew what, whatever.

Verna came in, though. She looked pale and kind of like pudding and didn't talk about any of it. Bonnie stepped outside with her and they had a few words, but it was just between them and not for repeating.

When Verna wasn't around, the opinion in the store was pretty much fifty-fifty as to whether Roy was gone for good. Con Stephens said Roy had an eye for the skirts, and Tunk Smith opined there were enough of them over in Bar Harbor. Carl Henry said Verna had a heart of gold and you wouldn't find that every day in Bar Harbor. Ralph Audry said it wasn't a *heart* of gold that Roy was necessarily interested in. Bonnie said there was no way in any event Verna was ever taking that bastard back, and of course she spoke with the authority of having talked to Verna personally, even if she wasn't repeating any of the particulars of that. Mac said some people seemed to be forgetting that Roy smashed up Verna's *boat*, for Christ sake. Old Everett's boat, Lewis Early corrected. But opinion was still fairly evenly divided as to whether Roy was gone for good, because, as Burt Cummins put it, you never knew with lovebirds.

And of course the whole question was tied up with the other question of whether Verna should or should not have sold to Mr. Bloch and whether she could still change her mind or if she'd lost her last chance and the wisdom or damn foolhardiness of all of it. Ralph Audry remembered his father telling him about when the Hubbards had the largest spread on Clement's Cove. Mac said you couldn't go by that, if you went by that, then the Indians originally had the largest spread on Clement's, the Indians had the whole spread, for pity's sake. Ralph said he wasn't talking about the Indians. Mac said of course he wasn't talking about the Indians, that was just his point.

But Tom Benson and Tunk Smith kind of agreed with where Ralph was going with his opinion, it was kind of like honoring the past, what Verna was doing.

Carl Henry felt it was more about the money and Verna was just being shrewd to hold on and someday what she had would be worth a whole lot more even than two million dollars.

Burt Cummins firmly disagreed, he said you could look at a whole history of prices in the Town Hall and of course everything had gone up a ton and probably would continue to, but it would be years and years, maybe even after Verna's time, before prices caught up with what Mr. Bloch was offering for that little tiny bit of Verna's. Since he worked over in Town Hall, Burt was listened to on this.

Nobody had much to say about Mr. Bloch or Mrs. Bloch, except that she wasn't apparently going by Mrs. Bloch, she was still Miss or Ms. Whatever-she'd-been-before, which Bonnie had heard on *Oprah* was getting to be a thing of the past. The assumption seemed to be that when people have that kind of money it's hard to know much about them. Nobody, at least not now, was condemning Mr. Bloch for making the offer. It was just a little weird, that's all, a little out of the shape of things. Though, as Ralph Audry put it, there were a lot of things out of shape these days.

Bonnie did come up with one confirming piece of fact. Mr. Bloch was indeed a Jewish fella. Not that that had anything to do with anything. It didn't, Mac said, but he sure had a lot of money.

CHAPTER 10

BLOCH WENT BACK TO HIS NEW YORK ARCHITECT. The New York architect brought up a team of landscape architects. The landscape architects brought in a geologist from Portland and soil experts from Camden and everyone brought their engineers and there was a pool designer too. More lawyers were hired to advise on the coastal laws. A plan came into being. The pool would be sunk in the high narrow spine of the land and it would run north and south as the land ran, and so that its scar on the land could not easily be seen, trees almost as big as those that would have to be removed for the construction would be brought in and planted when the construction was done. It was all tremendously expensive. They began blasting the ledge in November.

Once the decision was made, Bloch moved on. They were living in the city, in a loft on Greenwich Street north of the Trade Center that was as large and comfortable as the co-op apartment on Fifth Avenue that Maisie had grown up in. Maisie did the decor herself. She was afraid of decorators. Throughout the winter she took care of her girls, took them to museums and the little park by the river and entered them in "Mommy and Me," and the rest of her time she spent reading and throwing a few pots and taking classes and going to the gym, not so much to regain her strength any more, because she'd done that, but to keep herself strong. She still did a bit of yoga. She believed in nothing, she might say to you if you asked, but when she said it you might look at her and think she still believed, or once again believed, in the possibility that life was good.

I might put in here that Maisie had once been my lover. For a little while and in an odd circumstance. We were both members of a quasi-esoteric group, with a leader, in New York. In the late seventies, and I'd loved her like a comrade, and then she took up with the group's leader, and then it all fell apart. I've written about that part of our lives. After the group, we drifted apart, and Maisie went out to Taos and opened a breakfast restaurant, and had lovers and her twenty-minute marriage and more lovers but the years to have children went by, and then when she wanted to there were problems with conceiving, because of the Hodgkin's, the doctors said. So she adopted her two little girls from Hubei province, China, and gave them names from her family, Alexandra and Margaret, as if by doing it there could never be some dotty aunt who would question where they belonged, and then she met Adam Bloch on a New York street.

Bloch was done with business now, though if you made the billions yourself you're probably never really done with it. There are still managers to pay and papers to sign and reports to review and philanthropies to found, and you must be polite to people who are suitors for your money, who want it for this or that, to make more money with it or to give it away. Bloch allotted two hours of his day to his money. He still felt modest about it, really. He didn't live the way other billionaires lived, or the way he read about them living, anyway. He didn't really know. He didn't know other billionaires, except maybe a few from his various businesses, and those were about business and he didn't pursue their acquaintance anymore. He had never had many friends.

Now he played his cello every day. He gave it two hours, like his money. He took walks with Maisie and the girls or took the girls out for ice cream or went sometimes to the museums with all of them. Did that fill up his days? Not really. He tried to become interested in politics, but mostly failed, though he felt the impeachment of Clinton was an outrage and gave more money to the Democrats then. He built an art collection of contemporary pieces that he didn't entirely like, and was thinking of trading them all in for Mughal miniatures. Often he longed to be back in Maine, to sit on his oversized porch and watch the water or see how the construction of the pool was getting on or walk into the general store and have ordinary people say hello to him. He would call up somebody every couple days, the architect or the engineers, to see how the pool was coming. When there was news, he would tell Maisie.

A lot of their life was like that, telling each other little bits of news. They went to functions together. They spent their evenings together. They had sex, say, once every week or sometimes every two, and mostly in a desultory fashion. It was not a marriage of passion, he knew that from the start. Or what was he talking about? It was a marriage of *his* passion.

As for Maisie, she wondered, quite often, if this could last or how long it could last. She didn't consider this a disloyal question. She wasn't "bailing out." She just wondered, the way she imagined anyone would if they'd scarcely been married before and were in their fifties and life was exigent and complicated and possibly short. She liked Adam. She found his naïveté, his modesty, his instinct to do no harm, to try to leave the world no worse for his having been here, endearing. Especially because he had done harm, and he knew it. Harm to her, harm to everyone she loved, and even if he had done so inadvertently, it had left a stain. He was like a man doing a penance, and for some reason Maisie found this to be one of the acceptable ways of being in the world.

A simple conversation they had once:

"I'm sorry, Adam."

"For what?"

"I think you know for what."

But really he didn't. Not then, when she said it to him, when the girls were put to sleep and they were sitting quietly each with their books and their thoughts, in the library she'd insisted he build for himself, that had a window looking west, across the river and into the night.

Later it dawned on him that what she had said was like a template for a conversation that could have gone exactly the other way. He should have said, "I'm sorry, Maisie." And she could have said, "For what?" And he would have said, "I think you know for what."

Would that have made him feel better? Would that have been a better way of doing it?

Even falling in love, for Bloch, was something like a penance. He married the sister of the girl he killed. Though he would remind himself not to say it that way, not to place more blame than he could bear. The sister of the girl who died in the crash. There. Was that better? She came from the best of families. She was fiery in ways that he could never be. She filled in the missing pieces of himself. Her red hair flew around. She was or had been sick and needed taking care of. She wasn't intimidated by all the money. She knew a million things he didn't and she had a million graces he lacked, so many that she could throw them away, profligately. She had lived a life without nets, had even cut the ones she was born with. She was a little crazy, and he was surely not, he longed for the champagne of madness. She was the sister of the girl he killed, marked out to him like a blazing star by fate.

They stopped work on the lap pool in January on account of the freezing conditions but they resumed in March and Verna saw again the stream of trucks and trailers going up and down Bloch's road. Bloch was told there had been delays. The weather, the frozen ground. Now they were shooting for the end of the summer. Bloch was a patient man himself, but to his knowledge Maisie wasn't. Reluctantly he became a boss again, he asked questions and where he found the answers silly or implausible he fired a few people, just to show the rest that such a thing was possible. He put off telling Maisie but finally he did, he told her that the pool wouldn't be ready until fall. She shrugged as if for a moment she'd forgotten it was being built at all. "There must be a YMCA up there somewhere," she said.

CHAPTER 11

Roy came to regret what he had done. He argued with himself about it, because he was always regretting things he had done, Roy recognized this as a pattern in himself, do something one week, regret it the next, and then sometimes he would act on his regrets, and things, instead of getting corrected, would go from bad to worse. But regarding Verna there was no way he couldn't see how he'd screwed up. For one thing there weren't a whole lot of other girls coming into his life. Freddy had all kinds of girls on the side but Roy didn't have any on one side or the other. You could see the difference between him and Freddy when sometimes Freddy would pick up two girls for them and both the girls would pay attention to Freddy. Roy couldn't figure it but there it was, sometimes you just had to face the ugly facts. Freddy just had a way with the skirts, it was like he could always think of something funny to say, whereas Roy could think of things to say but they usually weren't funny. Secondly, concerning Verna, there was no way he should have busted up her daddy's boat, that boat meant a hell of a lot to Verna and it was just a mean drunk thing to do. And Verna wasn't a bad old girl, to boot. The one thing that had nothing to do with Roy's weighing process, as he saw it, was all the money Verna was supposed to get for her land, since after all she wasn't getting it. Roy decided the first thing he'd say to her, if they ever got back together, was that he respected her decision vis-à-vis Mr. Bloch, and that would be the end of that discussion so far as he was concerned right there.

Roy felt actually it would be a considerable sacrifice on his part to say this, since at the moment there was no question that he could use the money. The thing with the Queen of Italian Cuisine had finally gone to court and wound up costing him fifteen hundred dollars, once you added the lawyer's fee on. But more than that, Freddy was about to launch an expanded operation that had an excellent chance for success. Royce Gilmore, who owned the largest limousine operation in the eastern part of the state, had passed on in February and his daughter who got the business had decided to slim down operations and was selling off a portion of their vehicles. Freddy knew the owner of the lot in Ellsworth where they were being consigned and had negotiated a knock-down price for all of them sold together, which he was offering Roy a fifty-fifty percentage piece of, provided Roy could come up with the proper funding. Roy was flat busted himself, the only thing he owned was his pickup truck that was five years old with a hundred ten thousand miles that he still owed the bank on. But he wasn't going to tell Verna any of this. If it came out later, fine. The one thing he wanted to communicate to her in the first place, and he would do this in no uncertain terms, was the fact he was sorry.

Verna took Roy's apology under advisement. He just came over one day and told her how he'd screwed up. The weirdest thing. She heard an engine sound outside that sounded like his truck, but she'd been mistaken so many times about that on account of all the trucks going up to Mr. Bloch's place that she wasn't even going to look. She took a peek through the curtains anyway, because she always took a peek whether she wanted to or not, and there it was. Roy told her how he'd screwed up and was sorry and would make efforts never to fly off like that again or go drinking to excess, and also how he respected her decision vis-à-vis Mr. Bloch and that it was the end of that discussion as far as he was concerned.

Roy certainly *looked* sorry enough. He brought over a dozen and a half carnations from the Tradewinds and his eyes didn't dart around like they sometimes did, like they were eager to be out of a situation—this time they either looked straight at her or at the floor. She told him that what she worried about was compliance, i.e., if he'd do what he said. He said he could only do what he could do. Verna couldn't argue with that. Roy could see things were going in his direction just by the way she couldn't find the next words she wanted, it was like she was in the process of changing her mind but hadn't thought up the words to do it yet. He figured to close the deal by telling her how messing up Everett's boat was something that if he personally ever wound up being God, he'd for sure send himself to hell for. He hated to say that but it was true. It was the worst thing you could do to a man's memory and his daughter, but he intended to fix the boat like new.

"I don't believe you can," Verna said.

"You think I don't have skills, Verna?"

"I think you've got skills, Roy. But I don't believe you can."

"Then we'll just have to see."

Roy had a toothy smile, a little lopsided as well, that could seem brave sometimes. He was defying her doubts now, and she remembered that about him. Roy had a certain kind of confidence, which Verna so far lacked that when she saw it in someone else, even if it seemed more stupid than brave, and likely as not to wind up like a busted dream, she couldn't quite ignore.

This time Roy moved in. He'd never moved in before, though he'd spent any number of nights a week there. He brought his clothes over in a box. That was about it. His tools he kept in his truck. He quit paying rent on the place over in Sedgwick, and that was surely a help. A portion of what he used to pay over in Sedgwick, he gave to Verna for his share, and that was also a help, in terms of keeping things on an even keel with her.

Most evenings Roy spent over in the lean-to with old Everett's boat. He decided it wasn't in as bad a shape as he remembered. He spent a lot of time looking at what needed to be done and then he set to work. Measure twice, cut once—everybody said it, but you couldn't deny it. Then he consulted with various persons, Tom Benson in particular, about the best way of getting the new planks bent to shape and certain other aspects. He'd once helped his own daddy build a boat, smaller than this one, more a dinghy, but it had been lapstrake too, and that's what he was otherwise going on, his memories of that. That was his ace in the hole which gave him the confidence to say anything to Verna in the first place. It had been the choicest time he could remember with his father. They took a whole summer and when the old man wasn't fishing they built that dinghy.

Verna watched Roy's progress with interest. Tom Benson came over to look at the progress sometimes and Tom was saying it was a helluva job. What Verna noticed mostly was that when Roy was through for the evening, he'd come over and be in the sweetest mood. He must have been proud of himself or something. It used to be that nights he'd spend a lot of his time complaining, about the various things you could of course complain about, the weather and money and people from away and what the state was telling you you had to do or couldn't do now and the way they made it hard on people with any initiative or ideas and what somebody or other said or was said to have said, about himself or about something; or he'd be scheming, coming up with his ideas and already upset because they were going nowhere. Now he'd come back to the trailer and have one beer and they'd watch the news and the sports and more often than before, before they went to sleep, he'd be in the mood for a little more.

Things went on this way through the mud season, and Verna began to hope she had a new man on her hands. She began to hope he'd never finish his project of rebuilding her daddy's boat. In the meantime there had been delays with the limousine deal that Freddy had negotiated. It was an on-again, off-again thing, one week Royce Gilmore's daughter wanted to slim down operations, the next week she didn't. But by the middle of May she'd finally made her mind up. Freddy was salivating. That's how good a deal it was, fifty percent off blue book. Finally it was putting pressure on Roy: in or out. Of course his answer would have to be out, as things currently stood, but he was still hoping for some version of a miracle. One night when they were particularly getting on, he decided he ought to at least mention the deal to Verna, just to see what she would say. He picked up some lobsters from the Marine and an oversized bottle of wine and when they were done with a hands-down outstandingly delicious meal he broached it with her.

Roy's eyes radiated the purring excitement he felt when this whole issue came up in his mind. They were little boy's eyes. He didn't know how else to put it, he said. He felt she should just be aware. But if people were going to make something of themselves in this part of the world, they had to take their chances where they could get it.

"You mean, Freddy." Verna, as expected, did not think highly of Roy's prospective business partner.

"I know you don't think he's too high class an individual."

"He's proved that," Verna said.

"He's just a real character," Roy said.

"So what is it this time exactly?"

"You know if you're going to have an attitude going in, what's even the point of me telling you anything?"

"Tell me, Roy. Really. I want to hear."

So Roy told her about Royce Gilmore and his daughter and the slimming down of their fleet and the limos halfway below blue book and the deal Freddy had negotiated with Peterson's Cadillac in Ellsworth and the whole idea of a fifty-fifty split, which would give Roy something in the world at last. He laid particular emphasis on the market research that Freddy had carried out to make sure there'd be demand for all these limos. His market research showed there'd be plenty of demand, there was pent-up demand, it was a case of if you build it, they'll come.

"What kind of market research?" Verna asked.

"What do you mean, what kind?"

"I mean, did he hire somebody, or what? He just go ask strangers in the street, would they like a limo ride?"

"Why're you being so cynical, right from the jump here?"

"Well you said, 'market research.'"

"I don't know exactly what kind, okay? Okay?"

"Okay. Fine. Then how much money would you have to put up?"

"Forty thousand dollars."

"Forty thousand dollars?"

"Forty thousand dollars, what's wrong with that, that's peanuts, for a half share in six limos? Fifty percent off blue book, you could take 'em down to New York and just sell 'em for a profit that way, if nothing else worked out."

"You don't have forty thousand dollars, Roy."

"That's correct. I don't."

"Well then . . ."

"I just thought you should be aware. I didn't say I was going to do it. See, this is a perfect example, you're always telling me I don't tell you stuff. And right here, here's stuff. Don't seem to make you any happier, if I tell you everything."

"I'm happy you told me, Roy."

"Are you, Verna?"

"Well it's good for me to know what you're thinking about, isn't it?"

"It's why I told you. I wasn't asking you to put up the money yourself."

"I don't have forty thousand dollars, Roy."

"I meant, making that deal with Mr. Bloch over there."

"You're still thinking about that, aren't you, Roy?"

"I'm not *thinking* about it, Verna. It's not like I'm *thinking* about it. But it's a hard thing to put out of your mind totally, you'd have to say that."

"I still think about it," Verna said.

"Do you. Is that so?"

"It's like you said. It's not like I *think* about it. But it's kind of hard not to."

"All I meant, if you wanted to do something. If you wanted to be in on this deal yourself, by any chance."

"I don't."

"Of course. Absolutely. I didn't think so. But if you did. See, I wasn't thinking any more like you'd sell your piece. It's more like, you go to the bank, you say this Mr. So-and-So offered me this for my property, so I guess that's what it's worth now, so you get a loan out on it. That's all I was talking about. One of those home loans. Not even a mortgage, just one of those home loans they got now. Not that you'd want to. I'm not saying you should."

"I already got a loan out, Roy."

"Is that right? I didn't know."

"So I couldn't take out more."

"If your place was worth more, because of this Bloch guy."

"They're going to know, just like you said, it was a one-time thing."

"Well anyway it don't matter, since I'm not getting you involved in this."

"It's not a question of *me* getting involved. It's a

question of *you* getting involved in some knucklehead idea which wouldn't be the first of Freddy Belliveau's knucklehead ideas that turned out to have a joker in it someplace. Just think, Roy. Just think. Why would the daughter be selling off the limos, if there was a demand for them out there?"

"Why didn't Royce Gilmore sell 'em off then? He's the one knew his business, and he didn't sell 'em, he just dropped dead, he couldn't help himself."

"I still say, she's got the established business. You're going up against that. What if she takes your money and goes out and buys three new limos? Then where'd you be? She's got the superior cars *and* the established business."

"You know you're thinking like a business person here, Verna."

"No way. It's just common sense."

"I mean, with that kind of business acumen you're showing here, I'd go fifty-fifty with you myself."

"You're bad, Roy."

"But let me just answer this question, okay? Because it's a good question, it's a smart question. And actually it was the first thing I happened to ask Freddy and he went and we asked and the answer is, she's pulling out of Mount Desert Island altogether. She's living over in Old Town, it's too far for her to Mount Desert, that's why she's slimming her operations down. Mount Desert's going to be free territory."

"She gonna put that in writing?"

"Aw, Verna. Jesus. Expect the Almighty to bow down to you, expect assurances about every single thing. You got to take some things on chance, that's just life, Verna. You never believe anything, where are you?"

"Well . . . one thing I would say . . . there's plenty of rich folks on Mount Desert Island."

"Of course there are. Of course there are. You got the Rockefellers, you got a million people. Hey, Freddy's not exactly going broke over there, and he's only got one vehicle."

"I'll tell you what I do think, Roy. Every person should have one chance one day. It's only right."

Verna got up to put the lobster shells in the trash and get out the ice cream. Roy was curious about those last words of hers, but he chose to say nothing. He'd learned enough about Verna to leave some things alone. You get as close as you can get to something, and then you don't press it, you don't blow it. It was a rule he was trying out, anyway. It was something Freddy had told him. Freddy had read a number of books about management.

In the days that followed Verna did some online research concerning limousines and the demographics of Mount Desert Island and the overall economic conditions of that part of the county and she made some discreet inquiries of a few of the folks she cleaned house for as well, and in particular Mr. Elliot, who'd been in banking and all of that prior to retiring to Clement's Cove. But Mr. Elliot didn't know much about limousines. He never took them himself. He said he figured the summer folk over there, if they were anything like around here, which maybe they weren't, but if they were, a limousine service might be a little bit spiffy and a little too like the cities they left. On the other hand, there was all the traffic at the airport and they'd have a superior product to the Bar Harbor taxis, and maybe if they converted a couple of the limos so they'd be more like touring vehicles, bright colors, et cetera, take out the smoked windows, lemonade in the minibar instead of hard liquor, there could be a whole second line of business, a fun way for people to see the coast. Or join up with one of the steamboat operators, a half day of that, a half day in the limos, which Verna interpreted as a kind of surf-and-turf of tourism.

She had a lot to think about. Late in the afternoons, when she was done cleaning but Roy wasn't home yet, she'd go over to the lean-to to consult with her daddy's boat. It wasn't speaking to her now. It sat there like a boat. It was starting to look the way it used to look before Roy bashed it all up. He was at the point of sanding the whole hull down and starting over with the paint, and it looked kind of like a naked version of itself, like Verna almost wanted to wrap it in a blanket. But it made Verna happy that Roy was working on something her father had worked on, even if the reason for all that work she'd rather have forgotten. It showed how even a catastrophe could in proper conditions turn into a good thing. It showed God's working, in a way. Or maybe it did. Verna wasn't sure, but she had hopes in that area, as she had hopes now that when Roy was finished working on the boat it would be what she had not believed possible, it would be just as it was the day that Everett died.

And as for the trailer and the land and the money and Mr. Bloch's offer, Verna began to recall how close she'd come to taking it in the first place. It was only that scruple about her father's wishes that had stopped her, and she couldn't hear that scruple now. Now she thought about how, if she sold her land to Mr. Bloch, the money that Roy would need would be only a tiny, minuscule portion of what she would receive. She would hardly notice it was gone. She could help Roy and it wouldn't hurt her at all. He could even blow it all and it would be a disaster and he'd feel terrible and admit that Freddy was a jackass and someone he would never listen to again, but she could forgive him. Easily she could forgive him. She could tell him that it was the right thing for everyone to have one chance one day. The only dread she felt about any of it now was what if she was too late? Or, no, of course she was too late, the trucks were going up and down every day, what did Mr. Bloch need with her land now? Unless he simply wanted her land. Unless it would make a tidy package for him. Or maybe, and this was just a vain hope, she'd heard about the delays they were having. The delays might mean trouble. The delays might mean Verna still had her chance.

CHAPTER 12

WHEN BLOCH HEARD THAT VERNA HAD CHANGED her mind and now wanted to sell him her property, he was faintly annoyed. He had gone far out of his way and made choices he hadn't wanted to make when she said no in the first place. He had spent as much time as he wanted to spend on the question. He was happy that things were now proceeding on an even keel and that when he and Maisie returned to Clement's Cove on Memorial Day he could go over and check up and be like the sidewalk engineer that a few times long ago with his father in downtown Pittsburgh, like a boy in a *New Yorker* cartoon, he'd thrilled to be. There had been delays, but they seemed past now. And anyway, the delays made him only more reluctant to change his course. If he dropped what he was doing now, after so much effort and so many delays, people would only think he was a fool times two. They'd call him money-crazy. They'd call him indecisive or neurotic or worse. Bloch wondered if they ever called people neurotic in Clement's Cove. It didn't seem quite right. It didn't seem like what they would say. But it would be what they meant.

Of course there was the alternative of leaving the pool where it was and just acquiring Verna's plot as a kind of mopping-up operation. There was even a certain rationale to it, to buy the last bit of land on the head that wasn't already his. He of course wouldn't pay her what he had offered her before. That was past. And it had anyway been a moment of childish desperation. Bloch could see such things in retrospect. He got crazy because of Maisie. He would become crazy again for her, he knew that much about himself, he would do crazy things as many times as were necessary. But they weren't necessary now. He didn't even mention Verna's change of heart to Maisie. He felt it would only upset her. He was afraid at any moment she would throw off Clement's Cove and all of it, and then where would he be? Maisie was volatile. This was an article of Bloch's faith. Everything he had done here was to tether her to the earth, or really to him, as if he came along as part of the bargain, Adam as part of the earth.

It was a straightforward business proposition, really. When Adam was at sea, his instinct was to revert to the thing he was good at. He might be clumsy with feelings and dull of speech and he blinked too seldom and his mouth could go dry with longing or regret, but he could make sense out of things from a business point of view.

The money, in absolute terms, meant little to him. *Monopoly* money, really. But he felt he must at least try to make it mean something to him, just as he must at least try to shut off lights when he walked out of a room, not out of compulsion, or for nostalgia's sake, but in order to keep life in a proportion he could recognize. His business sense told him that Verna had a powerful motive to sell now. It also told him that her land was worth a quarter million dollars at most and that he could get it for half that, he could get it for almost anything he wanted to pay, but he oughtn't to pay too little because that was not how business worked. Business, if you were a man like Bloch, meant cultivating a reputation for fairness. Take the last dime out of a situation and you might be a princeling today but you were a dead man tomorrow. Act as though there were honor to the whole thing, clothe the wretched beast in velvet, and the world won't run away. Bloch the honest broker. It was shtick, but it had always worked. Having a head for figures wasn't a bad thing, either. Bloch remembered, with an embarrassed regret, that he still liked to play *Monopoly*. But these days he was careful not to play to win.

He went so far as to talk it over with Jackman the lawyer. What to offer. How to phrase it. Whether to move her trailer for her or buy another plot for her. The things that had been in the air before, when he needed it and was crazy. And Bloch might have gone through with it, might have made Verna a tidy little offer for her land, but for the fact he got a flat tire driving home from the lawyer's office in Bangor. He didn't even know where he was, except that he was north of Route 1. It was a landscape of marshy springtime fields and rolling hills and a stream meandered through the fields and Bloch remarked to himself there could be worse places to be stuck without cellphone service. He stood in the road and waited for passersby and waved at the first pickup truck to come by. His was a slightly rueful wave, as if he felt foolish to be in this situation and sorry to put anyone to the trouble. But the truck pulled over anyway.

The driver was bulky with a reddish beard and small eyes set like peas in a ruddy face and he wore a T-shirt that made a joke about black flies. He asked Bloch if he had a spare. Bloch said he wasn't sure. Bloch offered him twenty dollars if he'd change his tire. The guy said he wasn't going to be changing anything if Bloch didn't have a spare. He rooted around in Bloch's trunk and came up with a half-sized tire that he showed considerable contempt for, as being what the car companies believed they could get away with these days. Bloch nodded and watched the guy work. The guy kept up a patter about various subjects both related and unrelated to what he was doing, the nail that got Bloch's tire, the prevalence of nails and such on roads where there'd recently been construction, the piss-poor cellphone service north of Route 1 generally speaking, and what it would have cost Bloch if he'd had to call a tow truck, which he explained to Bloch as, "They'd of got you by the shorties, my friend. They'd of jew'd you pretty good."

When he was done the guy repacked Bloch's jack neatly where it went and dumped the flat in the trunk and Bloch paid him the twenty dollars and the two men went on their ways. Bloch was grateful for the guy's stopping and for the good-natured part of him and the honest way he'd worked, and all these made it harder for Bloch to forget the guy's opinion as to how the tow-truck operator would have treated him if the tow truck had got there first. "Jew'd you pretty good." Bloch told himself the guy wouldn't know a Jew if a Jew foreclosed on him.

Yet he would drive a couple of miles and the remark would come back, like a road sign around a bend. Bloch hated himself for letting such a thing turn his eye. Remember the blacks, the Jews' old rallying cry, meant if for nothing else to put things in perspective. And all the rest, the AIDS victims, the gays, the transgenders, the lesbians, the Puerto Ricans, the Mexicans, every minority you could name, as if lined up in a silent army, like the terra cotta soldiers of Xian. This country was good to the Jews. "Jew'd you pretty good," unconscious, almost sweet, in the ordinary course of things. Yet Bloch found himself crossing Route 1 as if hoping for a return to friendly territory. And when it didn't work, and he still remembered? Vaguely, Bloch sensed himself on the wrong side of a bright divide, with the guy in the pickup and Verna and most everyone he knew around here, even Hayward Jackman the lawyer, even Cord, even Maisie, on the other side.

The desire to be a victim or the yearning not to be. The push and pull of every man's life. The shadows, the echoes, of the millennia. Did people believe in ghosts? Bloch resented being played this way, or playing himself this way, or whatever it really was. He who didn't believe in ghosts, who believed, still, in the possibility of reason.

He remembered what Cord had said about Verna. The Hubbards had been around a long time. And it didn't matter the circumstances, some day she, or her child if she ever had one, or somebody, or everybody, would hate him for buying her out. He couldn't chance that. He didn't even think it was right to chance it. He could see that now. He was on the wrong side of a bright divide, but every bet he had made assumed the opposite. Or at least the possibility of the opposite. He would act as if it were all true. He would be the champion of Verna Hubbard's land. He would protect it even when she in a weak moment wouldn't. He would prove something even if he couldn't say what it was. He would never buy Verna out.

CHAPTER 13

VERNA DIDN'T WANT TO TELL ROY THE BAD news. It was the worst part of the bad news, really, having to tell it to Roy. She couldn't even get herself to cook a meal to make it softer. He came home and it plopped out of her like an egg.

Roy sat in the Naugahyde lounger that had been Everett's with his knees apart and a beer. He'd not been anticipating this. He'd told Freddy good things were cooking. But now that he heard it from Verna's lips, he wasn't surprised at all. Not one bit surprised. The only thing warring in him was why he wasn't surprised. On the one hand, there was the fact that every time one fucking stinking half-assed opportunity to give him half a leg up in life came along, it turned immediately or soon enough to shit. Roy tugged at his beer and considered this to be God's truth. Almost thirty-five and he was never going to catch a break if he lived to be a hundred and six. That's how some people just were born, their lives stank, and no amount of perfume or sweat or ideas or anything they did in their whole fucking existence was going to change the outcome of that one iota. On the other hand was the possibility that this was all Verna's fault. After a couple of beers, while she sat there with him in the half-dark with neither of them saying much, he decided maybe it was the second thing.

Finally he said to her, with some circumspection, "So. Did you come back to him with some kind of lower offer?"

He'd been silent so long, Verna was caught unawares. "What offer?"

"Didn't you make an offer in the first place?"

"I just told the lawyer I changed my mind. I told him I'd sell."

"Jesus, Verna. You got to make some kind of concrete offer with these things. You can't just leave it in limbo."

"It wasn't up to me to offer. He's the one offered, in the first place."

"Yeah, but you're coming back to him now. You got to show you mean business."

"Roy, he just said no. I'm sorry. But he did. He said no. It's not my fault."

"I'm just talking tactics. You got to have tactics. For instance, okay? I thought of this. I'm not saying you do this. I just thought of this. But let's just say he says no. What kind of cards you got to play, Verna? You've still got cards. You're not tapped out. By any means. And this is just what I thought, for instance. He's got a nice place there. He's got millions in, rich people coming and going, right? Right by your own place, which they can see. So say he says no. The next thing, just for instance, you start messing up your yard a little. Why do you have to have the neatest mobile home in Hancock County? Obviously, you don't. You leave stuff out. You leave the garbage can out. You forget to mow the grass. Any number of stuff. You make your place an eyesore."

"Roy, that's horrible. You're crazy."

"It's just tactics, Verna. I'm not saying forever. It's just tactics. If he's going to say no, you do something back."

"I'm not making my place an eyesore."

"It was just for instance, okay? The point is, you don't just take this lying down."

"I'm not taking anything lying down."

"Of course you are. What do you call it, then, what you're doing?"

"I'm not aggressive, that's all. It's no point."

"How do you know, if you haven't tried?"

"You want to call the lawyer, Roy? Go ahead. See what he says. You call him."

"Well maybe I will."

"Be my guest then. Just don't go telling him you're going to trash my place."

So Roy took over the negotiation. The next day he called Jackman and left a message that he would now be representing Miss Hubbard in the possible sale of her land.

Two days later Jackman called him back, on Roy's cellphone line, and said his client wasn't interested at this time but he would get back to him some time in the future if his plans changed.

Roy hated this formality of tone. He took another tack and said that Miss Hubbard understood Mr. Bloch's position, going ahead with the pool and all, but surely there were other considerations regarding the possible value of the land to Mr. Bloch, and Miss Hubbard was prepared to be reasonable and understanding in terms of price. She wasn't out to make a killing, she just wanted fair value.

Jackman expressed appreciation for Miss Hubbard's reasonableness, but repeated that his client's interests were focused elsewhere at this time.

Roy thought Jackman was a fucking asshole by then. He decided to go specific, just like he'd advised Verna, and said her property could be had for a half million dollars cash.

Jackman said thank you and that he had another call coming in, and hung up.

Roy called back two days later, but Jackman didn't return his call.

Roy decided he'd at least try this thing of trashing Verna's yard. He left a bag of garbage by the road one night and the raccoons got it and then the crows and the garbage was all over. Verna went to pick it up but Roy stopped her. She said he was a fool. He said, okay, he was a fool, but he was in charge of this negotiation now and she at least had to give him a fair chance, he'd clean up the garbage himself later but just let it sit there for now.

Verna got teary and said she'd rather not sell at all. Roy said he could understand how she felt, and if she truly felt that way he'd desist as of now, but it would be the end of his dream. Verna hated him for saying that, but the garbage stayed in the road. Somebody from Bloch's place came down and shoveled it up.

The next night Roy put out more garbage and left his truck up close to the road instead of down the driveway and since it wasn't supposed to rain he put his tools out all around Verna's yard, as if he planned to plant them or something. The next day he put her old barbecue out in the driveway and a blue plastic beach float that had a hole in it and some other stuff that even a garage sale would be ashamed of. Verna had given him five days to make this work. On the fifth day he called Jackman again. When Jackman picked up the phone, Roy felt his tactics must be having their intended effect. He was almost giddy with expectation. He wasn't going to give in too easily. He was going to get Verna good money for her land.

But all Jackman had to say was that his client intended to call the Town Hall if in the near future Miss Hubbard didn't come into compliance with the local zoning on refuse, unless there was some excuse, such as illness or being away, that his client was unaware of.

Roy said he was unaware of any problems or of Miss Hubbard being out of compliance. But maybe there was an alternative compromise that could be worked out, Roy said. If Mr. Bloch truly didn't want Miss Hubbard's land anymore, still he might want an expansion of his right-of-way on the road so that he could plant trees and never have to see Miss Hubbard's trailer again.

Jackman laughed and said his client liked seeing Miss Hubbard's trailer.

Roy refused to believe this. He said that for only eighty thousand dollars Mr. Bloch could have the expanded right-of-way and a screen of trees and never have to worry about Miss Hubbard's refuse problems again.

Jackman promised that he'd relay the new offer to his client. He felt duty-bound, he said, to convey new offers to him. Roy took heart in this. He told Freddy things were coming together. He took Verna out to Deer Isle to dinner. Two days later Jackman called back and said no. Roy reduced his offer to sixty thousand, then to fifty, then to forty, but Jackman still said no. His client just wasn't interested.

Verna fixed up the front of her trailer so that it was prim and decent again. Roy hated her for doing it because it reminded him of his defeat. But then, if she'd left it all untidy, that too would have reminded him of his defeat and he would have hated her for that too. He recognized this. He was a man who could recognize things in himself, for good or bad. He was ashamed of himself for blaming Verna for everything and vowed on the day that one fucking thing, like even the smallest tiny fucking thing in the universe, turned out right for him, he wouldn't blame her anymore.

CHAPTER 14

IN THE GENERAL STORE THE FEELING PREvailed that Verna should never have waited so long if she wanted to sell her land. Strike while the iron's hot, somebody said. A bird in the hand, Carl Henry said. A case of don't count your chickens, Tunk Smith said, but it turned out he was ribbing the others on account of their clichés. In general, people blamed Roy. It continued to be a wonder to Bonnie that Verna took him back in the first place. But Tom Benson said he was doing a nice job on the boat. People forgot that about Roy, he said, he was a fella who could do things when he put his mind to it.

"What mind?" Bonnie cackled, and there were a couple of other people's guffaws that trailed along with her. But no, seriously, she said, it was good for Verna to hold on out there, it was the guts thing to do and it was only Roy who had talked her out of it to start with.

Roy with his big ideas and that criminal friend of his Freddy Belliveau.

Lewis Early asked why was she calling Fred Belliveau criminal and Mac said you just don't go calling people criminal with no evidence.

But Bonnie stuck to her guns, pointing out the incident with Francesca Romano and what she heard from a friend in Southwest, namely, that during the eighties Freddy smuggled marijuana over there.

If he never got caught, then it's only suspicion, said Tunk Smith, who'd had similar suspicions raised about himself in the past concerning his ability to support his ex-wives. Allegations only, Carl Henry said.

And anyway who cared, Con Stephens said, none of it had beans to do with Roy anymore, because Freddy had gone out and got himself a new investor. This was what Tom Benson heard, too, straight from the horse's mouth, Roy himself told him that Freddy was romancing some summer person over in Northeast Harbor to invest fifty thousand dollars. That was last week he told him, and Roy had seemed pretty upset.

But he shouldn't be, Burt Cummins said, Freddy was doing him the favor of his life, not to get him involved in such a shaky scheme as that one.

You never knew, Mac said, with a business proposition you never knew.

He knew, Burt Cummins said, Freddy and his limos were a loser, and in fact if you went to New York City these days, they hardly even used limousines any more, they got these *town cars*, that's what people wanted now, *town cars*, it just showed how little Freddy or Roy knew about anything.

Bonnie said her feeling still was that Verna ought to kick Roy's butt back over to Sedgwick. Who'd she go out with then, Ralph Audry asked, did Bonnie have any bright ideas, considering she was so quick to be busting up people's relationships. Bonnie had to admit that at present she didn't. So that's the whole story in a nutshell right there, Lew Early said. Tunk Smith, who for some reason was considering himself the cliché police today, said nobody better say that beggars can't be choosers.

As for Mr. Bloch, it was no surprise to anybody that he no longer wanted Verna's land. It just made sense. He'd gone in another direction. The consensus in the general store, as expressed by Mac, was that Mr. Bloch was more worthy of respect for not buying Verna's land than he would have been if he bought it. It showed he wasn't interested in coming here and just buying everything up.

CHAPTER 15

MOST OF THE SUMMER PEOPLE CAME BACK TO Clement's Cove for the Fourth of July. They came to air out their houses, see friends, relax, and act a little silly, or nostalgic, or unsophisticated, or immature. They came to make sure their children had the childhoods they remembered or had never had. The parade, the fireworks, the tug-of-war and three-legged races, the burnt cheap hot dogs from the Tradewinds, the odd phenomenon of seeing grown men and neighbors walking around in red, white, and blue pants and top hats, the party at the beach. It was the start of the summer. Coming back to Clement's Cove for the Fourth of July was like standing up for the kickoff at the Harvard–Yale game.

Maisie had a vicious migraine, so it was left to Bloch to take the girls to the beach. He took them by their hands and they walked down the road. Bloch felt like an ersatz patriarch, a father in disguise. Could this really be him, with those little hands in his, holding on with the excitement of dear life itself? When he had first met Maisie's girls, he could hardly tell them apart. Now he could tell you hundreds of things about each of them. Alexandra was sturdy and tall and impulsive and she learned how to swim the first time she touched water and screamed when the TV went off and liked artichoke leaves and broccoli and was starting to read and loved any animals that were larger than herself but not the little ones so much. Margaret had delicate bones and coughed every winter and drew perfect little drawings of the things in her world, she concentrated and scrunched her forehead up and when she was done there was a purple flower or a bunk bed that looked just like a purple flower or the brand-new bunk bed and she never complained about anything, even about her sister who could try to boss her but couldn't really, because Margaret was too busy and careful and inward to be bossed. Hundreds of things more, at least. Go on. Let him bore you. Let him start taking out the pictures from his wallet.

Sascha. Maisie sometimes called Alexandra "Sascha." Maisie's sister's name, her sister Alexandra, whom everyone had called Sascha. Bloch walked down to the beach with Alexandra and Margaret gripping his fingers and he felt honored even by their names. The life he had chosen to live or the life that had chosen him. Sascha. One day, perhaps, he would call Alexandra "Sascha." For a few minutes they stopped by the road so that all three of them could pick berries.

One odd thing about the party at the beach was that Bloch knew more of the Mainers than he knew the summer people. By their faces, anyway, or by their nods, alternately wary or deferential or matter-of-fact, when they saw him coming into the store or the post office or walking along the roads. There was Verna, of course, and Mac and Bonnie, and Burton Cummins from Town Hall and Con Stephens the contractor and Thomas Benson the plumber and then all the others who'd worked on the house or the pool in one fashion or another, so that Bloch was embarrassed to think he might have been the employer of people he didn't even recognize. Not that that meant a helluva lot in Clement's Cove, to be the boss. People did the work they did, which was the best that they could do, and if you didn't like it you could find somebody else and see if they'd do it any better. Bloch liked it that way. He liked Clement's Cove. But still it felt odd how few of the summer people he could even nod to. Melissa and I were away. Cord was around, but he was dishing out hot dogs like a Southern carnie tout and didn't have time to talk, beyond shouting out the girls' names and giving them the fattest dogs he could find on the grill. Or that's what he said he was doing anyway. To Bloch they looked all the same size.

And anyway it hardly mattered to Bloch, on this day that seemed to propose country innocence, whom he knew and didn't know. The point was for Alexandra and Margaret to make friends. The three of them wandered by races that Bloch had never seen before and didn't quite understand. They hung out by the cotton candy. They went back to see how Cord was doing. But Cord's kids were all grown. High school, college. One at Yale. Maisie's girls, even Alexandra, seemed a little shy today.

And then the boat came in. Something unexpected, not only for Bloch but everyone else. Roy had put old Everett's boat in the water to test it and when she tested good he decided to put her to decent use giving the kiddies rides on the Fourth. Everett used to do it himself on the Fourth, not in this boat but in his old boat that he fished in, so Roy was just carrying on a tradition. He figured if nothing else it would win him some points with Verna, and it did. It made him seem to her as if he liked children. And who knew, maybe he did, and he just didn't know it before.

Roy very nearly beached the boat. He brought it in so close that kids could climb aboard just by taking off their sneakers and socks. He shouted he was giving free rides and every kid who wanted one should just line up. Pretty soon there was a fat line of little kids and big kids, summer folks and locals, that snaked up the beach above the tide line. Roy was a hit. With its scarlet paint so fresh, the boat looked almost like a toy put in the water by some local giant for its amusement. And Everett's old sixty-horse Mercury, that Roy had declined to send over to Danny Creighton for a rehab in favor of working on it himself, surely sounded enough old and cranky, but on the other hand Roy had got it going, which was believed to be something of a feat unto itself.

Bloch watched the ragged lineup of shorts and baseball caps from a little distance away. Alexandra asked if they could go on the boat. She said she wanted to, but for her part Margaret wasn't sure. "Let's watch it go first," Bloch said. And so they stood their little distance away, on a patch of ooze and mussels, and Bloch was relieved when the girls for a few moments turned their attention to the gathering of shells. Bloch wanted to see if it was all a legitimate and safe operation, Roy and his boat and his renovation. He wanted to see as an ersatz parent whether this was something he should be permitting.

The depth of Bloch's ambivalence surprised him. To go in this boat or not. To risk Maisie's girls or not. To trust the world or not. It began to feel as if his whole new life was at stake, and if he failed he would be back where he had been, back somewhere he could hardly any longer remember. Roy was passing out life jackets now, but they were old, bleached, flimsy things, the kind that once upon a time had been bought at a discount store or an auto parts store, the kind you'd get if you thought life jackets were a silly thing to start with. Though Bloch corrected himself, criticized himself: they were also what you'd buy if you had little money. Still, they looked flimsy, and he saw Roy putting one on a girl who was Margaret's size and it was so big on her it could have floated off her. Everett Hubbard's old life jackets, probably. Bloch knew little about life jackets, but he didn't like the look of these.

He knew little about the water, either, but he could see beyond the cove and it was not yet noon and the froth of late afternoon was already out there. Bloch didn't know. He wasn't sure. He let the girls look for shells while he continued to watch the little bright red toy of a boat.

Roy must have filled it with so many kids because the line was long and he didn't know how else they'd all get a chance. Ten kids, a parent or two, and Roy, so that they all wound up standing up or sitting on the little foredeck or the rails. Verna pushed them off. The Mercury labored under its load and the boat meandered out of the cove as if seized with half-heartedness. But then that must have been a ploy on Roy's part, to save a thrill or two for down the line, because as soon as he cleared the head, he gave the Mercury full throttle and Bloch could hear its sharper groaning and see the toy boat banging itself against the waves and then it disappeared.

He wasn't sure how long it was gone. He didn't check a watch. The girls tired of gathering shells and Alexandra still wanted a boat ride, so in the end they got in line. But it was still a very long line and they wouldn't be getting to the front of it anytime soon. Bloch was concerned now with the boat's repair. He had heard how Roy had smashed up Everett's boat and how he'd built it back together, but had anyone checked to see he'd done it well? As far as Bloch knew this was its maiden run or its next-to-maiden run and he could see the whitecaps out there, and whether the work Roy had done was good enough in a battering sea was another version of the question that was turning Bloch this way and that as if he were already in the waves.

Just a question, he didn't know, nor did he know who to ask. And he didn't want to be made fun of, either. The flimsy jackets, the froth, the overload of human cargo, the maiden voyage, the repair, the groaning old Mercury motor. Bloch wondered what Maisie would do. It was a clear day and Bloch could see no fog anywhere, but thirty years ago on the weekend that Maisie's sister Sascha died in the crash he'd gone out with his friends in a boat from Clement's Cove and there was no fog then, either, but the fog had come up quickly and surprised them. Roy's boat was gone for what seemed like a very long time. He was probably taking them all the way to Cape Rosier and the open bay. What would Maisie do?

She would tell him to decide for himself, of course. She would tell him to use his judgment. She would assume he knew what to do. She might even assume or hope that if the boat got in trouble, if it capsized or hit a rock or the engine failed or a wave swept somebody off the rail that Bloch would have some clue as to what to do. But why would she assume or hope that? Who did she imagine he was? It was another factor to consider.

In fifteen minutes the little scarlet boat came around the head and again into view. When it reached the shore there was laughter and chatter and the people on the shore observed and remarked that nearly everyone on the boat was soaked. The flimsy life jackets were exchanged. Another load piled aboard. Roy couldn't get the engine restarted. He yanked at it and tweaked it and took the cover off and tweaked a few things more. Bloch watched his frustration grow, until it reminded him of the phone calls that Jackman had received regarding Verna Hubbard's trailer from this same Roy Soames. They had seemed so pathetic, in Jackman's telling of them, that Bloch had almost given in. But Roy was a whiner, Bloch decided, and he didn't trust whiners.

Finally, Tom Benson took off his shoes and waded to the stern of the boat and gave Roy some suggestion, and whatever the suggestion was, it got the old Mercury going again. By then Bloch had decided to take the girls home. He told them the line was too long and that Maisie would be wanting them home for lunch, so they left.

"Why, though? That's what I don't understand." Maisie was recovered from her migraine. It was later in the afternoon. The girls in their room napping, Maisie and Adam on the porch, in fleece jackets with their hands in their pockets because the fog had just come in. Light on its feet and stealthy, it slipped over the porch rails like a burglar and blew in whispers down the porch.

Bloch stared at her, unable to blink. He wasn't sure if he'd done wrong or been done wrong. He wasn't even sure if he could get out words. "It was that combination of things," he managed to say.

"But the whole point was take them over so they could see some kids, meet some other kids. They've got to do the things kids do here. They can't be like freaks out here."

"I know that, Maisie."

"I mean, we've got this enormous house, for four little people, it's ridiculous, I grew up like this, I don't need this, don't you get that?"

"Isn't that another subject?"

"I just want them to have a normal life here. *I* want to have a normal life here. And if you're going to be scared of every little thing, if you're going to act like a person can't catch a cold because it'll be the death of them or whatever that stupid thing was people used to say, when maybe it would be the death of them back then, but it wouldn't be now. You're just so scared of everything, Adam. Where does that come from? You're going to drive all of us crazy."

"It was just a judgment call. Really. I'm sorry. But if you'd seen that boat . . ."

"I have seen that boat."

"And?"

"I don't know. It floats, doesn't it? It didn't sink, did it? I mean, people around here know about these things. Believe it or not, they're scared of the water. A lot of these people, especially the old ones, they don't even swim. They know if a boat's not safe."

"You're probably right. I probably should have just done what they did. . . . But the fog did come in."

"Jesus. Jesus. Yes. Now it's in. How many hours later?"

"I was just trying to do what I thought you'd do. And I still think, if you'd seen what I saw . . ."

"Wrong. No. Wrong."

"What about when . . ."

"Don't start with examples from the past, alright? Don't start with stupid examples from the past, because, you know, you're so logical, you think you can just be totally logical and that's all life is, just figure everything out, in that little mind there. You know what you're like? If somebody bashed you in the head, a lot of clock parts would come out."

"Thank you."

"Don't thank me, even sarcastically."

"Well what do you want me to say, Maisie? I already said I'm sorry."

"I just . . . I don't want to be a freak. I don't want my girls to be freaks. You brought us here. We didn't have to come here. But now that we're here . . ."

"I thought this would be a good home for you."

"Yes, yes, okay, I like it here, okay? But I don't want to be a freak."

"You're the one wanted the lap pool."

"What in Christ sake has that got to do with it? Oh for God's sake! It's only a lap pool. Is that such a big deal? Okay, forget it, tear it out, don't finish it. I'll go to the Y."

"There is no Y."

"You know what I'm saying."

"I'm sorry what I said about the lap pool."

They were quiet after that. But everything Maisie said had been building up in her. She had said all of it before in different ways. But it had built up again.

Now she wondered if it was not, in fact, a little freakish on her own part, a little contributing to the delinquency of a timid rich guy, to want a lap pool dug in solid ledge on the coast of Maine.

But what Bloch said slowed her down anyway. "It's my joy for you to have what you need."

They were quiet again. Bloch rued sounding so eloquent. It sounded stupid to him, the sound of his hoarse words seemed to linger in the damp air of the fog.

Like a lie? Was that the miasmic shape his mind made in the mist?

If so, Maisie didn't seem to notice, and Bloch asked himself, further, if he had gotten away with one, if he had talked her into something that even he didn't believe.

"You know what this fog reminds me of?" she said.

"What?"

"When Sascha died. That was in the fog, wasn't it?"

"It was."

"I think that's what you're afraid of. I think you're afraid of . . ."

"Repeating it? Doing the same thing again? Killing somebody?"

"Am I wrong?"

"I can't . . ."

Suddenly Bloch felt as if he were choking. He looked away. He stared into the fog's blankness.

"What?"

"This is a problem. This is my problem, you see."

"What's wrong with you? Are you okay? Adam, look at me."

"Why?"

"Why? Look at me! Jesus."

So he did. He looked at her and again he didn't blink.

"I'm sorry."

"You can't be sorry all the time."

"But I am."

"You'll kill us all then."

"There was fog, yes. There was fog. The night Sascha died. Am I speaking clearly enough now? That night, there was fog."

"Adam, you're not scaring me, you know that, don't you? You're just being a shit now. Just come back here. Come back here."

"I'm here," Bloch said.

CHAPTER 16

MAISIE WANTED HER LAP POOL TO BE PLAIN. She didn't want a spa or a fountain or waterfall or rock formations or black tiles or a vanishing edge. She wanted it to be as unadorned as the chlorine-faded tank suits that she swam in. That was her aesthetic. That was her choice. If she was going to scar the land, she wanted the scar to be as honest as possible. She wanted a mark simple and geometric and severe. She didn't want it to blend in. She wouldn't have believed it if it blended in. She didn't want to swim in fantasy.

Bloch had a bit of a time conveying this idea to the builders and designers. They'd keep to it for awhile, but then have some idea that this or that adornment would be a nice touch, or an interesting highlight, or just something that an expensive pool shouldn't be without. They couldn't quite accept the idea that something so expensive might not look it. It was beyond being conservative, it was beyond tasteful restraint, it was just plain, and it irritated them and even made them think that others, future customers, would think that Bloch had been overcharged. How could you put so plain a pool on your Web site? In truth, Bloch wasn't unsympathetic to the idea of having a few flourishes of observable luxury. Did the tiles from Saragossa that each cost as much as a caviar tin really have to be the color of sand? But they were what Maisie wanted. Bloch felt that she could see things that he couldn't.

The summer went along. The last summer of the millennium, by some calculations, the second-to-last according to others. Bloch, being a rational man, was inclined to be in the second-to-last camp, but who was he to argue with the popular mood? It was a time that seemed peaceful enough. Presidential blowjobs still at the top of the national agenda, stock markets going nuts, a country struck dumb with its overall good luck. Maisie put the girls in a "pre-day camp" and went every day with them to make sure they didn't cry. For herself she found a heated public pool in Castine and drove over there in the late afternoons. The house began to be a little more lived in. They expanded the frontiers of what they used. When she thought of it, Maisie even bought stuff. And the Elliots would come over or they would go to the Elliots, and they met others over there. Women who were fighting the Wal-Mart with Denny, sailing buddies of Cord's. Clement's Cove was sweetly boring and quiet, so that you could hear yourselves think or laugh. Maisie read a biography of Tolstoy. Bloch read Gibbon. Both of them read to the girls.

Like a watchdog Bloch kept track of it all. Maisie's moods, the girls' moods, the progress of the pool. He wanted it done by Labor Day. They were promising that it would be and by August he began to believe it. Extra crews arrived. Crates with tiles and filter equipment and heater parts arrived. It was all coming together.

And perhaps it was only because it was all coming together that Bloch's darker imagination began to sense Maisie's indifference to it all. She made remarks about how she liked driving over to Castine, the pool was cold there but she was getting used to it, she liked getting out of the house. They had babysitters by then. Phalanxes of babysitters, and for next year Maisie was thinking of an *au pair* from Hungary or Slovakia, or maybe a pair of *au pairs*. Bloch liked it that she was even thinking of next year. But her indifference, if that's what it was, to the lap pool annoyed him. The fickleness of women, all of that. Bloch was not immune, he realized, to feeling the chronic complaints of men. The age-old complaints of men.

It became a subject he didn't discuss with her. He just wanted the damn thing done. It made him anxious wondering if she'd like it or not or if his darker imagination was betraying him or not. August could be anything in Clement's Cove but this one was warm. On the long dry days the workmen raced toward their finish line. On the eighteenth of August the general contractor knocked on the door and told Bloch that the heater and filter were hooked up in test mode. The tile work wasn't done and the coping needed its finishing grout, but the pool was full of ninety-degree water and if anyone wanted to try the thing out they should make themselves feel free.

Bloch hesitated to tell Maisie. It was late afternoon and she'd just come from her swim in Castine. And he wanted this to be perfect now. He wanted the pool to have its best chance with her. She who, Bloch believed, believed in first impressions. Although, if that were entirely so, how had she wound up with him? *Pecunia omnia vincit?* Maisie came out of the kitchen and asked him who had been at the door and Bloch told her it was Falsey the contractor and the pool was heated to ninety degrees.

He let her go up the path herself in a terrycloth robe so that he could watch her disappear into the woods. In Bloch's modest understanding of it, Greek goddesses were always disappearing into woods, and he liked considering Maisie that way, an eternal something in a terrycloth robe. Nor did he want to seem to be following her around, or to be on the scene as if waiting for instant praise. Instead he sat on the porch. Whatever would be, would be. Silly thoughts, boyish thoughts.

Maisie threw off her terrycloth robe and took the plunge. The pool was so warm she thought she would have to tell Bloch to turn it down. It had to be ninety-five degrees. Adam had a way of going overboard, she thought, as she swam her laps. She was a little tired from having just swum an hour before, but the water, as usual, gave her its own good reasons to keep going. Her life was this now. Her life was swimming laps. Until she was done, and floated on her back, and saw the spruce rise everywhere around her like giant blades of dark grass and the sun glinting through. Maybe not a sacred glade, but close enough. The plainness of the pool was to her liking. It was there because men had come in and put it there.

In an hour she came back down the path in her terrycloth robe, her damp hair stringy and dark with chlorine in a way that seemed happy and used, and reported to Bloch that everything was terrific, except the water was a little too warm.

Bloch smiled reservedly, the way he'd learned to smile, in good news and bad, afraid he'd seem a fool to show how happy he really was. As soon as she was gone inside, he ran all the way to the pool himself, threw off his clothes down to his underpants, and in a moment of astonished joy, jumped in.

CHAPTER 17

Something more about Maisie. She liked to get to the bottom of things. She didn't stand on ceremony, didn't keep her mouth shut. But Bloch was not so easy. That talk on the Fourth of July. The fog, his fear. It was not that she thought she was telling him anything new.

Crazy girl. Talking therapy. Labels that didn't apply. All her life, it seemed.

In her own humble opinion, winding up as sane as anybody else. And maybe saner, so go fuck yourself. Life had made her sane. As best she could figure it out, anyway. And occasionally keeping her eyes open.

She felt, or sometimes hoped, that she rounded out Bloch's life with sincerity. She didn't lie to him. Not much, anyway.

Had she married him because it was easy? No real answer to that one, except if there were fools around who thought any marriage was easy. But then the question wasn't whether marriage was easy but whether marrying him had been easy, and what if it was, but there were other things as well?

Had she tried to tell him that the reasons for his self-contempt were not real? Of course she had. She had *told* him. As if telling were the same as living.

The girls. The girls, the girls.

If she prayed for anything, Maisie prayed for time.

CHAPTER 18

THINGS HADN'T BEEN GOING ROY'S WAY. HIS fallback position was going to be that when Freddy closed the deal with the summer person from Northeast Harbor and got his expanded fleet of limos going, Roy could at least drive for him. A bitter pill, considering that until recently Roy had been hoping to be Freddy's partner in the business with a full half share of the profits. But at least the tips would be pretty good if you drove a limo on Mount Desert Island and the hours would be to his liking and he'd be away from the Clement's Cove area where in his opinion people had gotten into the habit of scrutinizing him a little too much. And now that wasn't working out, either. The summer person from Northeast had backed out of the deal. Freddy wasn't getting his expanded fleet after all. He was in almost as bad a shape as Roy was.

Roy did odd labor around, for Con Stephens and Tom Benson among others, and some of that labor was even for Mr. Bloch himself, as an employee of Con Stephens he'd done some hauling away of pool debris. The whole thing galled him. Getting paid so much less than Con Stephens and Tom Benson galled him, when he was every bit as smart as they were and wound up doing the heavy lifting for them. But more than that, this whole thing with Mr. Bloch and his pool and his house and his wife and all the people working for them in various ways and everyone saying he was a nice enough fella and a fair enough individual to work for while Roy for his part could put two and two together. For instance, why couldn't Mr. Bloch come up with this lousy forty thousand dollars to protect his view from Verna's trailer? It was a fair deal, you couldn't say it wasn't a fair deal, Roy wasn't trying to gouge him. And he could sure afford it. And it could have solved all Roy's problems.

Not that Roy expected a stranger to solve his problems. Roy wasn't that crazy. But still. There was something Roy couldn't put his finger on but he knew he didn't like it. The money. For safety's sake, just call it the money. If you had so much of it you probably couldn't even count it, why be so fucking careful with it? Although, of course, the simple answer to that, what everybody said, was that's how you got to have more money than you could count, by being careful about it. There. That was it, that was what he was trying to put his finger on, that was what Roy didn't like. He felt this person ought to be freer with himself.

And the swimming pool, too. Nobody'd ever built a swimming pool in Clement's Cove before, nobody'd ever felt the need to, and least of all in the middle of a pile of rock. Days when he wasn't working Roy would be out in Verna's yard, splitting wood or fooling around with Everett's boat, and he'd watch the trucks go up and down the road and he'd think to himself, God almighty, what a fuss over nothing. Hadn't grown men got better things to do with themselves? He even made a bet to himself, that Bloch wouldn't swim in it once himself. He didn't look like the swimming type. He told Verna. He told her he'd bet her, too, but she didn't like to bet.

So Roy didn't take it well the night Verna suggested to him he ought to go work for Mr. Bloch.

"Why don't *you* go work for him then?" Roy said.

"I'm not the one needs regular work, Roy."

"I got work," he said.

They were watching the antiques show on the public station, which Roy couldn't stand, but which Verna got a kick from every time somebody that looked like herself found something in their departed aunt's attic and it turned out to be something like Abraham Lincoln's walking stick. She liked the way they all cried a little or covered their mouths when they found out what it was worth.

"Look at that thing. What is that thing?" Roy in his transparent change-the-subject mode, almost making fun of himself for changing the subject, because it looked like Verna was starting on a tear. "Looks like a dildo to me."

"It's an old pencil sharpener, Roy."

"They have dildos back then? Sure looks like a dildo."

"Jesus. Roy. Could I have that please?"

She reached across him and the lounger for the channel changer and muted the sound.

"I thought you liked this crap."

"I'm talking to you about something."

"I told you, I got work."

"You're standing around here two-three days a week. That's not work. You call putting little tiny dabs of paint on Dad's boat work?"

"No, that's not work. That's leisure. That's my leisure time."

"Suit yourself then."

"Well I am. I'm waiting on a number of situations."

"In the meantime, you sit around complaining, Con Stephens is ripping you off, everybody's ripping you off. I happen to know because Marla told me, Jimmy Phillips was getting twenty an hour up there for general labor, just general labor. Because he was working for Mr. Bloch instead of those blockheads. No middleman, Roy. It just makes sense."

"Why'd you mute the sound out?"

"So I could talk to you."

Roy again looked disgusted at the TV screen.

"What's *that* thing?"

"What's it look like, it's a picture. In a frame."

"Yeah, of what?"

"Roy."

"You go up there, Verna. You add a client."

"I don't have room for another client. Believe me, if I did, I'd be up there."

Roy pretended once more to be interested in the antiques show. After awhile he muttered, "Shit."

"It was just a suggestion, Roy. Don't be mad. Would you not be mad, please?"

"Shit."

It didn't occur to either Verna or Roy that Bloch might not hire Roy because he didn't like him or had already formed a negative impression of him. If anything, Roy felt, Mr. Bloch would have recognized at least his entrepreneurial spirit. Three days later, after enough time had passed so that Verna couldn't think he was doing it in response to her nagging, and because, as Roy put it, a few of the situations he was waiting on appeared as though they might not pan out, Roy went up to Bloch's place to apply for work. Or he didn't apply exactly. Roy made himself available. He went right to the front door and knocked. The wife came to the door. Maisie. Roy introduced himself, said he was living down the road, cited the variety of his skills, and said if they had anything for him he'd be happy to consider it.

Maisie liked Roy's looks. The gappy smile, the shock of hair, the lanky athleticism, even the bad country complexion. He looked like he could do what he said he could do. She needed help around the garden anyway, and there were some other things that Adam was talking about, handyman kind of things, and it was still summer when help was hard to find. So she said, "We'll hire you." Roy wasn't going to bring up the subject of compensation because it seemed tacky to him at this moment and he felt he'd be in a better position to negotiate once they saw him on the job, but she asked him what he wanted, so he had no choice but to say his normal rate was twenty dollars an hour. Maisie said that would be okay.

Later she told Adam what she had done. He connected the dots for her as to who Roy was exactly. Maisie couldn't see anything wrong with any of it. Adam said he didn't really care for the guy but on the other hand he didn't actually know him, and if Maisie wanted to give him a try, why not.

CHAPTER 19

THINGS HAD ALWAYS BEEN A BALANCING ACT WITH Roy. Everything had its good parts and its bad parts. For instance in the case of working for the Blochs, the money was good and you could save on gas because it was right up the road and it only took two seconds to get there. That cut your workday by an hour or an hour and a half right there. On the other hand, there was Mr. Bloch himself. Mrs. Bloch wasn't too bad. Mrs. Bloch, Ms. Maclaren, whatever she wanted to be called. Maisie. She said Maisie was fine. Roy was warming up to that. He'd called her Maisie a few times already. Mr. Bloch, the same way, said to call him Adam, but Roy didn't feel he truly meant it. It was more like something he thought he should say to prove he was a regular guy or something. But Roy felt he wasn't exactly. He held himself too aloof. It was like the identical case with his money, in fact it was the same thing. Maybe he meant otherwise, but it wound up so you never just forgot who was the boss.

Which of course it wasn't right to complain about, since he *was* the boss. But on the other hand it led to, or was combined with, the other thing, which was that even though he was the boss, you could never tell exactly what he wanted. He was so fucking polite all the time, it was like he was afraid to tell you. And when he did finally tell you, it could be so fucking stupid and clueless you'd wish he'd never told you in the first place. Verna was learning not to get Roy started on this.

Though there was one case he must have told her about twenty times. After Roy was done getting Maisie's garden ready for the fall, the next thing they wanted was Mr. Bloch had a big pile of videos and DVDs and television scripts, obviously from when he'd owned a whole TV company in California, and he wanted Roy to dispose of them. That was the exact word he used, *dispose* of them. There were boxes of them. They nearly filled the bed of Roy's pickup. Roy didn't even know what they were exactly until he drove them out to the transfer station. In fact it was Ralph Audry out there who was the first to see what Roy had and suggested there could be something of value there. So instead of throwing all the tapes and DVDs in a dumpster, they stacked them up in Roy's shed out at the transfer station. All the current hit programs were included in these tapes and a lot of movies Roy had never heard of, but then he wasn't one to keep up-to-the-minute regarding such things. They decided Ralph would sell them off at fifty cents or a dollar and the two of them would split the proceeds.

Then Callie Cummins bought a couple of these from Ralph and was in the general store with them and Mr. Bloch came in and apparently he could tell what they were because they were all marked "FOR YOUR VIEWER CONSIDERATION" or something of that nature. So now he came back to Roy and said, "I thought I asked you to dispose of those things."

"Which things?" Roy said.

"Those boxes of papers and videotapes."

"I did. I did that exactly, I disposed of them."

"Well I saw somebody in the store with some of them. Did you take them to the dump?"

"Absolutely. Took 'em to the transfer station and disposed of them."

"Well I don't know how, but I guess they didn't all get destroyed."

"Sir, Mr. Bloch, with all due respect, you didn't say *destroyed.*"

"I didn't?"

"No sir."

"Well could we possibly destroy them?"

If that wasn't the stupidest thing. Even there, he didn't say "destroy them." He said, "could we possibly?" Of course "we could possibly."

But anyway Roy destroyed them. What a waste. That's how Roy concluded the story, each time he told it to Verna. What a waste. Verna teased Roy at first about how he wasn't going to get to be Mr. Bloch's caretaker with that level of communication. But she found it wasn't a matter to tease him about. Roy didn't aspire to be a caretaker. Looking after damn fools, that's all it amounted to. To which Verna took exception, reminding him that Everett her father had been a caretaker fifteen years, after his retirement. Roy grumbled and said it wasn't for him, that's all he meant. He was going to start a proper business, as soon as circumstances allowed. It was the only way to get out of this situation.

It was past Labor Day now. A lot of the summer people had left. Adam and Maisie stayed on, but even they weren't there as much as they had been. Or she wasn't, anyway. She had doctors appointments in New York. She and the girls flew back and forth. While they were gone, Bloch found another job for Roy. Past Verna's place, as Bloch's road wound up toward the big house, there was a bend and it came out of the trees and there was a magnificent view to the south and west. The bay, the Camden hills, the islands. People had been going up there for that view when there was hardly a road. Now cars were coming up there all the time, which Bloch wouldn't have minded but the problem was that once they were up there they couldn't get out, there was no room to turn around and so all they could do was drive on up to Bloch's house and turn around in the circular drive, which meant cars were coming right to his front door at all hours of the day and night. Not a *huge* number, Bloch said, he didn't want to exaggerate, but enough to be annoying and a problem. "You have any ideas, Roy, how to solve that?" he asked.

"Let me think on it," Roy allowed, but by that same afternoon he was hard at work. He dug up a number of large rocks, of which there was no shortage in the neighborhood of Verna's trailer, and lifted them into his truck and drove up to where the magnificent view was and placed the rocks at three foot intervals all along there, so that cars coming up wouldn't even have place to pull off the road.

He was very nearly expecting a raise from Mr. Bloch on account of his fast work. He didn't see him for a couple of days. He had some brush-clearing to do and went at it. On the third day Bloch found him by the giant brush pile that he'd collected. "I saw the rocks you put out there," Bloch said. "On the road."

"You like that?" Roy said. "Nobody'll be parking there anymore, I'd estimate. The message'll be getting out."

"Well but here's a concern I have. The way it is now, if people stop anyway, they'll have to stay in the middle of the road, and there's that bend just past it going back into the woods. I'm just afraid it's going to cause an accident."

"If you're a fool enough to stop in the middle of the road, serves you right, I guess."

"I don't want an accident," Bloch said. "I don't want anybody getting hurt."

"Not too likely, I shouldn't think."

"Likely or not," Bloch said. "Have you got any other ideas?"

So Roy went back at it. He removed all the rocks from the side of the road and rolled them into the ravine. He went on to what he considered the next best obvious idea, putting up a gate. Not a big gate, not so delivery trucks and such couldn't get past. But enough gate to give people pause. He again set to work. He took measurements and began digging post holes for where he felt the gate ought to be. On his second day of working at it, he again observed Mr. Bloch strolling down from his house. He had a look of curiosity, like he just was wondering what was happening here. "Hello, Roy."

"Mr. Bloch."

"Really. Adam."

"'You say so."

"Look, Roy, what are you doing here exactly?"

"Laying the foundations. See if a gate can go here. Wouldn't do anything without your final permission, of course. And then too, you'll want to make your choice of gates, whether it's locked or not, whether it's one of these remotes or not, like a garage door opener in your car."

"Roy. I think I don't want a gate here."

"You think, or you don't want?"

"I don't want a gate here, Roy."

"Then how're you going to keep people out of your place? You said you wanted to keep people out of your place."

"I just don't want a gate. It's too, I don't, too something . . . too much."

"You're the boss."

"What about a sign?"

"I don't know if signs'll do the job."

"Well could we try it?"

So Roy went to the builder's place in Blue Hill and came back with an array of NO TRESPASSING and KEEP OUT and PRIVATE DRIVE signs in bright colors that would reflect at night. He staked them in the ground where Bloch's road began and further along the way as the road went up.

But Bloch didn't like these either.

"You know what they remind me of? Burma Shave signs."

"Why's that?" Roy asked.

"I suppose . . . there's so many of them."

"They don't say Burma Shave. They say keep out."

"And they're a little bright, the colors. And a little big."

"You said you didn't want people going up there."

"Couldn't we try something a little smaller? You know, plain wood, stained wood, or something. Just to remind people. I'd like to be polite about it."

"For pity's sake. You know what, Mr. Bloch? You don't know what you want."

Bloch smiled weakly. "Well I suppose there could be some truth to that."

"*Some* truth? That *is* the truth. I've done every damn thing but put a stoplight up here, and nothing's right, nothing's good for you. I don't know how to please you because I don't think you know how to please yourself, and that's the Lord's truth, Mr. Bloch. And don't say 'Adam.' Just don't say, 'Call me Adam.' I'm getting a little sick of this stuff. I'm getting a little bit fed up to here. You don't know what you want. And you don't know when people are steering you correctly. I'm afraid I can't help you any more, Mr. Bloch."

To make his point emphatic, Roy grabbed the nearest NO TRESPASSING sign that he'd staked in the ground, ripped it out and threw it down. "And by the way, you don't have to pay me for these signs or work on the gate or lifting all those fucking rocks. We're even."

Roy walked back down the road toward Verna's trailer, thinking this had been long overdue in coming.

When Maisie got back and he told her that Roy had quit, she was quiet about it. She didn't ask a lot of questions. Though in not asking a lot of questions, Bloch felt that Maisie was somehow taking Roy's side. As if Bloch had somehow provoked him. As if Roy was the one who lived around here and knew how things were done around here. As if Roy was somehow more of a man, younger and more full of life and a stabbing energy. She didn't say any of these things, but Bloch felt them in her silence. He might have been wrong, about her feelings, but he felt he wasn't wrong.

They began packing so that all of them would return to New York. She had too many doctor's appointments to keep going back and forth. And the girls' preschool would start in the middle of October.

The pool was finished now and Maisie swam in it every day.

Bloch solved the problem of the road and the unwanted visitors by posting a small wooden sign on a tree by the road on which was written, in letters that might sparkle a little at night but were otherwise undemonstrative, "Please Respect Our Privacy." Some paid it attention and some didn't, but overall the problem was less.

He slept not as well now. He would wake up after two or three hours of sleep and stare over at Maisie, who was curled away from him. He knew that if he moved toward her or touched her, she would not want it. She would hold still or whisper that she was sleeping or that she needed to sleep.

Cord Elliot had taken up hang-gliding and one day when Teddy Redmond was up from Connecticut, he invited Bloch to go with them over to Schoodic where there was a hang-gliding school. Cord and Denny had just returned from ten days in Marrakesh, Cord never having been one to sit around. Teddy had no intentions of going hang gliding himself, he had a foot afflicted with a touch of gout and anyway he simply wouldn't. He wasn't crazy like Cord. He would enjoy watching Cord fly around in the sky in a contraption that looked about as flimsy as some women's underwear. That would be enough thrills for him.

And when Bloch heard Teddy's intentions, he figured he could follow along in Teddy's wake, even if he had no touch of gout himself. Cord and Teddy were the ones, along with myself, who had turned on Adam after Sascha's death, who had been slow to forgive him and in some sense never could. These were facts on the ground, to Bloch and all of us, but also facts on the ground were the thirty-odd years that had intervened, and Bloch's generosity toward us all, and our mellowing, our ability to see around the corners of things better. The result being that we were all shocked and amazed yet on the whole happy enough, in a you-never-know-in-this-world sort of way, when it got around that Bloch had run into Maisie on a New York street and they had started dating; and felt more of the same when we heard they were to be married; and Cord welcomed them to Clement's Cove and so did I; and we stood up for him at his wedding, as if thirty-odd years had never intervened, as if once and for all we had become men. Always a tenuous proposition, always a test of faith.

Now Bloch was driving over with Teddy and Cord to Schoodic to watch Cord jump off a cliff, and Bloch was still a little afraid, as if there was something in him of the imposter, which in moments of sincerity, such as seemed called for by old friends, was in danger of being found out. The imposter that was in him, the imposter that was him, the imposter that was not him. Though he was content enough to be away for the day. Maisie was always going away, for a day here, a day there. She kept busy and she kept the girls busy. Bloch felt somehow that by going away he was lifting a bit of burden off her.

It was a familiar morning on the coast, that began with slashes of color and promise and soon clouded over with something more like the truth. A front coming in from somewhere. By nine the sky was gray and tense, as if the air was awaiting further instructions. Bloch sat on the hood of the car with Teddy and watched their friend float and loop around and rise in funnels of wind they could only imagine. He was like a birdman, like a guy with a crazy idea, distant, doing it, a speck suspended from blue-green wings between the hungry gray ocean and the bare glacial rises of the point. For a little while Bloch didn't think of Maisie. Cord as if representing them all, but what did he represent exactly? Their coming to the point in their lives where every solution was private. Get your money, fly your plane, build your house, get your kids into good colleges and if possible the same one you went to. And so it would go on, maybe. A matter of maintenance. But here was Cord, so high up in the air he looked like a little boy or a fool or a surprise. Being brave, in that private way. His friends had come along as if to keep the old days going, whatever those old days were, but Cord would have been there whether they were or not. Not a stunning victory. Maybe not even a victory at all. But something more than what Teddy's swollen foot or Bloch's skinny legs felt like as they dangled from the hood of the car. He came down out of the white sky like a messenger, slow and circling, landing in a burnt-over blueberry field. Somebody who had turned out well and did it make a bit of difference to the world?

Though, in the preceding paragraph, wherever I wrote *their*, I could as easily have written *our*. Our friend, our coming to the point of our lives, Cord representing us all. I could have been there, but I wasn't.

Although in another sense, I was. My understanding later was that through much of lunch they talked about me. Why the fuck *wasn't* I there? Where the fuck was I and who the fuck did I think I was, "going émigré" as if it were something akin to going postal. Good-natured enough. And Adam wouldn't have said any of that. Teddy and Cord, the ones that I was easy with. Bloch would have stayed silent. Though later when they wondered what I was writing and why I didn't e-mail and whatever else you could say about a guy who pulled up stakes for awhile, he might have put in a word or two. No hyperbole from Bloch. He could still sit and look like a rock.

Then they were all packed up and driving home and it was quiet except for the radio that Teddy kept fooling with, finding little that he liked. Bloch was in the back with Cord's harness poking around his ears. Most of the way Cord and Teddy argued about Bush, who was then a presidential candidate, and Bloch kept quiet. Cord seemed to be of the opinion that because Bush went to Yale with us and Gore who was sure to be the Democrats' candidate went to Harvard, that he would feel compelled to vote for George. After awhile he half-convinced the others that really, *really*, he was joking, but Teddy still suspected that if it ever came down to it Cord would vote for Bush. Bush had once nicknamed Cord "Third String," on account of Cord being Yale's third-string quarterback at the time when Bush was a cheerleader, and the year before I myself had been with Cord when Bush called up out of the blue asking for "Third String's" opinion about a businessman from Memphis who wanted some key post organizing for them in Tennessee. This was part of what made Teddy suspicious. And Cord saying that Bush was a "pretty good guy." He harangued Cord awhile about how it wasn't enough to be a "pretty good guy," if you were president you had to think of the world or for that matter they did too. It wasn't enough for anybody anymore just to be a "good guy." Obviously a cut at Cord, but what had Teddy done to save the world? Open a bike shop in Fairfield, Connecticut? Fail to get a script made or a book done in fifteen or twenty years? Things Cord didn't say, but Bloch the ever-neutral one at least thought them. Cord himself was still a good guy, and good guys didn't say such things to their friends, or if they did, it was with friendly sarcasm. Two roads diverging, but whose was the less traveled? Cord changed the subject.

Changing the subject was about as angry as Cord got. He asked Adam how things were going with Maisie.

Adam being in the back, his friends couldn't see that he didn't blink.

The question reduced itself to the stone that was inside him. He didn't know what to say, so he said fine.

"You packing up pretty soon?"

"Maisie's got some appointments in New York next week. More doctors."

"Anything going on?"

"Not as far as we know. Just checkups."

"That girl's brave."

"I think she is."

"We've got to have you over to the house before you leave."

"Good. That would be good."

Teddy hadn't had a word in, so over his shoulder he said, "Hey Adam, Mister Confirmed Former Bachelor, if I could ask as someone who's a little risk-averse himself, what's it like?"

"It's fine."

"That's it? It's fucking fine?"

"I guess."

"You know, you're a fine commercial for conjugal bliss, you fuck," Teddy said.

"Well. But it is."

"Maisie's one of the great ones. You got one of the great ones. And I've done some sampling."

"I know you have," Bloch said.

"Are you happy or not?" Cord asked. "That's all it boils down to." He'd become a little annoyed with Teddy's needling tone.

Bloch held his head up and looked forward between the seats, as if he had a bad seat at the movies. His neck felt stiff. *Was he happy?* His fear grew that he might do or say something unmanly. He who believed that once before in his life, and with these two men, he had done something unmanly.

Yet there was something matter-of-fact in Cord's tone, different from Teddy's bantering, that sounded like it might bear the weight of Bloch's soul. He began to feel the urge to answer. He asked himself, as if it were a question that could be put to him equally by an angel or a devil, what were friends for, after all. A cliché, a conundrum, maybe even a verbal sleight-of-hand. Bloch didn't really know what friends were for. They might have been for a lot of things. The one thing he knew was that he didn't want to lose the ones he had.

Although maybe it wasn't possible to lose friends. Maybe that was the thing about them, that they were impossible to lose. Bloch didn't believe that. It sounded to him like cheap propaganda.

Cord's simple question floated in his mind. *Was he happy?* Bloch felt like a sleepwalker and someone in the next room was calling to him, trying to wake him up.

"I'm happy," he said. His voice was hoarse, the way it got. Then he choked back quiet tears, which the others saw but said nothing about.

CHAPTER 20

THINGS THAT BLOCH MIGHT HAVE SAID TO CORD and Teddy.

That there were moments when he hated her.

That he had done no wrong.

That this whole thing with Roy and the signs and the gate and the pool and the house and buying and not buying and Clement's Cove was a conundrum.

That being rich was also a conundrum.

That he must remember to be grateful, that he must struggle to be grateful.

That it was worth the remembrance, that it was worth the fight.

That he was embarrassed.

That there were too few Jews in Clement's Cove, for a Jew like him, who was too much a Jew.

That you could scratch that last thought.

That Maisie was well, thank you, that the girls were well, thank you, that he was well, thank you.

That he hoped it would be seen one day who he really was. That even he would see it.

Or maybe it was all in his unblinking wet eyes.

CHAPTER 21

A DREAM OF MAISIE'S.

She comes out of the house. Roy is working in her garden and looks up at her with disdain or complaint. He stands up and says, "This disease won't grow." He repeats himself. "This disease won't grow in this soil."

Concerned, she asks, "Is there something wrong with the soil? If there's something wrong with the soil . . ."

She comes closer, to see what's wrong, what he's talking about.

"You're going to have to do something," he says, "you can't go on like this."

But when she leans down to look, it looks just like soil and she wonders why disease won't grow in it.

He smells like sweat and fertilizer.

She looks down at the soil and feels his fingers on her chin, lifting her face until she can see his gappy, happy, friendly smile, his hungry smile, his floppy, dirty, happy, hungry hair, and he says, "Sorry, ma'am, but my breath smells like fertilizer," and then his rough lips kiss hers.

A dream, of course, that she might not have had. But I believe she did. Some version of it, anyway.

CHAPTER 22

AFTER ROY QUIT WORKING FOR MR. BLOCH, the first problem that he knew he'd have to confront was how to tell Verna. He decided the best thing would be to get another job before he said anything to her. He even took the trouble of not looking for work around Clement's Cove, because word would get around. Instead he went over to Mount Desert. Unfortunately Freddy's situation over there had deteriorated from not too bad to worse. Not only had the summer person from Northeast pulled out of the purchase deal on Royce Gilmore's limousines, but Freddy's alternate driver had driven over some rough terrain and screwed up both the air conditioning and the transmission on Freddy's own vehicle. A big bill, in consequence of which Freddy was doing all the driving himself these days. And it was out of season now. Less demand for car service. Roy went a week without finding anything.

In the meantime he plied Verna with some nice gifts. More flowers from the Tradewinds, a nice little book on knitting that he saw lying around over on Mount Desert. Verna liked to knit. She'd knitted him a scarf once, which he'd appreciated and told her so. Though he also told her, at a certain point, that he didn't really wear a scarf too much, which had caused tears and her promise never to knit him one fucking thing ever again.

So in a sense the book was a little joke between them, or an apology of sorts, it was a present that had some thought behind it. And he also brought home half a side of beef one night. All this he considered to be laying the groundwork for telling her and softening the blow. But he knew he couldn't delay too long, because even though Verna left early for her appointments, she would sometimes stop back home during the day and Roy would soon be running out of excuses as to why his truck was never around or why she never saw him going to or from Mr. Bloch's anymore. And of course he'd be running short of money pretty soon.

He decided he'd have to broach the subject without having found new work. It seemed to him that over dinner, when they were enjoying a couple steaks that came off the half a side of beef, was as good a time as any. He began by reminding her once again of the stories that suggested how ridiculous a person this Mr. Bloch could be to work for. The videotapes and all of that. His analysis of Mr. Bloch was as follows: he must have been damn lucky to make all that money he had, because he sure didn't know how to make up his mind about anything, and in a business situation, decisiveness is the first thing that's necessary, you could read that anywhere, and in fact it just made common sense. So either he was just damn lucky or he used to have some decent sense and getting all that money just rotted out his mind and instincts, so that he was complete mush now.

Plus he was pussy-whipped. Totally pussy-whipped, in Roy's opinion, in fact, in back of it all, you could probably explain everything that way. Or the two went together. He had to ask *her* the difference between his ass and his elbow, and if she wasn't ever around to ask, he was in deep, deep shit.

"So you must be developing a lot of patience and tolerance to be dealing with all that," Verna finally said.

"I was. I definitely was."

"That's pretty good, Roy. I mean, that wasn't, that didn't used to be a strength of yours."

"But I mean, anybody, anybody at all, they've got their limits. Am I right? You can't work in a dehumanized environment forever."

"Now what's that mean? Dehumanized environment?"

"I'm saying, the man's an asshole."

"Oh, Roy."

"Roy what?"

"I hear you say things like that . . ."

"It's only the truth. The man's impossible."

Verna hesitated. Roy, perhaps, could see what she would ask next.

"Did he fire you?"

"Not exactly."

"What exactly then?"

"Verna, you knew this was always a short-term deal. To tide me over. Am I correct? That you knew that?"

"I couldn't but hope otherwise, could I?"

"That's very touching, the way you just said that."

"Are you being sarcastic?"

But his voice didn't have a sarcastic tone. Not then.

"You told him to fuck himself, didn't you? Or equivalent," Verna said.

"It wasn't like that."

"Oh no? Then what was it like? Tell me. I'd be interested."

"The man called me a stupid fuck."

"I don't believe you, Roy."

"That's your problem then."

"When did this happen?"

"When did what happen? It just happened."

"I just want to know, did it *just* happen or have you been hiding it from me all this time and being nice and everything, talking so nice all the time, and it was all bullshit again, all just more fucking lies, because you had something hard to tell me? You going to quit your contribution now?"

"To what? To the expenses? I swear, no."

"So you got new work, Roy? I haven't heard of you asking around."

"Well you know you could show some sympathy here, too. I'm the one's out of a job here."

"Did he fire you? That's what I want to know, Roy. Did he fire you? Or did you quit because you're such a big shot and know-it-all?"

"I'm not a big shot. I'm not a know-it-all. But I've got my pride, Verna. There's a big difference. Maybe you don't recognize that."

"Oh, bullshit! Bullshit, Roy! You quit ten days ago, didn't you?"

"As a matter of fact I did."

"I know you think I'm stupid. And I am stupid, okay? It was just blind stupid fucking bad luck, I was over to the Elliots' and Denny Elliot's on the phone with Mr. Bloch and she calls over to Cord that Mr. Bloch wants to know if Bill Mason's a good overall worker since he's looking for a permanent caretaker and Roy Soames just quit on him out of the blue. That was a week ago, Roy. So I've just been having a fine time since then, haven't I, listening all week to your lies. What a blast, figuring how you're going to get out of this one, which lie are you going to tell me next."

"That's nice, Verna. That's real nice, that's exceptional. See, you were just doing the same thing. Not telling me what *you* knew, that's just like lying. We're in the same boat, Verna, so get off your high horse, would you?"

"Fuck you."

She pushed away from the table so hard that Roy's plate landed in his lap. She didn't exactly mean to do it, but she didn't exactly mean it to not happen either. For a second, when the plate tipped off the table edge and Roy yelped, she felt her fear and satisfaction in equilibrium.

She went into her room at the end of the trailer. As soon as he put the plate back on the table and wiped his pants off, Roy followed her there to say he was sorry.

"Don't say that."

"I just did."

"Well don't."

"Verna, I've got plans, I've got dreams."

"You know you sound like the TV. 'I've got hopes, I've got dreams.' What are you, going to be in a stock-broker ad now? You going to be the truck driver who bought the dot com stock and now he owns the whole island? 'We can help you with your dreams.' All you've got are lies, Roy."

By then she was turned away from him, adjusting the photographs on top of her dresser, straightening them up a little. Frames three inches or six inches, her father, her mother, her sister and her sister's husband, her niece. None of herself, however. Verna noticed it, and it seemed odd, like a jigsaw puzzle with one piece missing, and why hadn't she noticed it before? She had such photographs, in a box in the closet, of herself with her father and mother, of herself with her sister, with everybody. They just weren't up there. Instead of thinking of Roy and where he was exactly, somewhere in back of her, Verna told herself that she should get some of those photographs out.

"What do you want me to do, Verna?" Roy said.

"Leave. Please."

"For what? For lying to you? For trying to soften the blow?"

"For being no good for me, Roy. I'm sure you'll be fine for yourself. I'm sure with your plans, all that'll be great for you. But as many times as you come back, you'll only be no good for me more."

Roy considered the possibility of coming up on her from behind then and kissing the back of her neck.

It had worked before, in a variety of situations, but he felt that it wouldn't work this time. And that realization, in truth, wounded him.

"You think I'm just no good. Even for myself."

"I just said the opposite."

"That's just to get rid of me, right?"

"No."

"Of course it is. I see that now."

"Go be sarcastic on your own time, Roy."

"What's sarcastic about that?"

"Go screw up every chance you ever get on your own time."

"You don't believe in me. That's the key here."

"Oh for pity's sake!" She turned to face him. Roy thought to himself that she'd never had a pretty face, even to start with. It had always been too big, and now that it was upset and glistening, it looked ever bigger. It looked to Roy like grief. "No," she said. "No, I don't, Roy."

He packed up and left.

Verna thought afterward that it hadn't made too much sense, what she'd said and done, she could even understand why Roy wouldn't understand it. It was an overreaction, in a way, because of all the times before when she'd underreacted. She viewed Roy, basically, as irreplaceable. That is, she didn't expect another to come along soon. But that was just how things were. She got out a few pictures that had herself in with the rest of her family, because it had seemed so odd to her that there were none out, and she got some more three-inch and six-inch frames the next time she was in Ellsworth, and put those up on her dresser along with the others. There was one of them where they were all in Everett's old boat. Not his red boat, but his old boat. Some kind of holiday. She missed Roy all the time, but felt she had to see this through.

CHAPTER 23

Because Maisie had to be in New York they missed the Blue Hill fair, but there was another fair in another county that Bloch wanted to take the girls to. A country experience. The cows being led around by 4-H boys and girls, the prize bunnies in their cages, the petting zoo, the cotton candy. The previous year, just before they were married, Bloch and Maisie had taken the girls to Blue Hill and it had been their peak summer experience, the one that might still occupy a happy patch of memory forty years on, and they had clamored and lobbied, as well as four-year-olds might, to go again. The only problem with the second fair, in Windsor, was that Adam and Maisie had decided to leave Clement's Cove for the season a couple of days before it began. More of her infernal tests. Getting the girls ready for preschool, getting their outfits together. Bloch decided to make Maisie a bold proposal. Bold only in this, that the one thing Maisie wanted complete and utter control of in her life was her girls. Yes, she knew it wouldn't go on forever. Yes, she was prepared, sort of, for the time when it wouldn't go on forever. But for now, they were her project. And Bloch had never spent a night with them when Maisie wasn't there. He had taken them to movies, he had taken them to concerts. Now what he wanted to propose to her was that she go back to New York and have her tests and he would stay on with the girls in Clement's Cove and take them to the fair in Windsor and they would join Maisie in New York two days later.

He was expecting she would simply say no. Or say something about how she needed the time with them to shop. Or even, if the going got rough, make some insinuations about how Bloch really knew little about children and wasn't prepared to deal with them for two days straight. He was expecting, in other words, to be disappointed, and to feel, as well, an absurdity in his disappointment. Here he was, a man who in business had directed hundreds if not thousands of people's lives, who had made or broken careers, whose every word was listened to, especially when his words were few. And Maisie would be telling him she didn't trust him with her four-year-olds. And that he wouldn't know what to do. Of course he would know what to do. He'd been around them all summer long. But she would not *trust* him. And the most absurd part: he would accept what she had to say, he cared deeply what she would say. He couldn't shuck it off. He couldn't say to himself he had another life to go back to.

Or of course, Bloch wasn't only anticipating such sentiments, he was already feeling them. He girded himself before he talked to Maisie about it. He felt his mouth go dry.

But it all came out the opposite of what he had imagined. Which just showed, when it came to certain people, and those people were women, the smarter you tried to be about something, the more likely you were to be wrong. Somebody had told Bloch that. Maybe Zacky Kurtz, the old producer of *Northie*. It wasn't something Bloch would have thought of on his own. His mind didn't work that way. Although maybe, he hoped, it was starting to. He at least remembered such things now, as if they were oddities he was beginning to collect from the human junk shop. He was becoming more normal, wasn't he? Such that when Maisie said sure, why not, and what a good idea that was, and she'd arrange for Joni the babysitter to come and help out, Bloch did not forget to blink.

This is why he loved her, he thought. Maisie could still be like sunshine itself. Her red hair and smile. Two older folks from very different places, but you cannot know where life will wind you up.

A sentiment Maisie might have concurred with. One day she felt like she was living with a stranger and another with a good friend, and yet he was the same all the time. So it had to be Maisie who changed. But if she changed, was it for better or worse? Was she just impossible to live with? Maisie tried to chart what she felt, after all, were glacial changes in Bloch. A growing confidence, a growing ease, a growing trust? When he proposed that he stay on with the girls and go to the fair, she had her misgivings but thought life had to be chanced. For once she was betting on him. It seemed only fair. Just as it seemed only fair, given that he was fair all the time, that she should be fair at least once in a while.

That night Bloch had a great misgiving. It didn't start as a misgiving, but then it was. Maisie was asleep beside him. A night unusually warm for the second week of October, so that she had put the windows open and you could hear the rush of the tide. Bloch lay on his back and thought of the brake light on his car. Or rather, into whatever he was thinking just before that, its flickering red light intruded, like one of those sudden interruptions you sometimes got on the radio, static and a booming voice, from the "emergency preparedness system," or whatever that thing was called. A reminder, doubtless, that a couple weeks before, on one or two occasions, the brake light of the Mercedes had flickered on and off. He'd had the brake fluid checked and possibly filled, but now lying in bed at midnight with the rush of tide in his ears he couldn't remember, if the fluid had actually been low, if at the service station they'd filled it. And what if it wasn't the brake fluid? Bloch struggled to think what else it could be. Rotors, brake pads, discs, as if words from a dialect other than his own. Bloch didn't know a lot about cars.

This was ridiculous, he told himself. Two weeks had passed. The light hadn't come on again. He'd had the fluid checked right away. He was driving himself crazy with false concerns, and only because Maisie had said he could keep the girls with him and take them to the fair. Bloch wanted to run this particular film in reverse, as in screening rooms when he hadn't liked something or hadn't understood something he could just tell the projectionist to go back. He wanted to go back to whatever he'd been thinking just before the red light came on in his mind's eye. It must have been something delightful, something about taking the girls. A petting zoo? A beautiful black-and-white cow with a prize medal around its neck? But he had no projectionist to buzz anymore, he was alone in this room with the windows open and he couldn't remember what it was. What it wasn't, for sure, was what he thought of now, which was the Blue Hill fair, not of the preceding fall when he and Maisie took the girls, but the fair as it had been at the end of the summer of 1966, when he had come to Clement's Cove with me and Cord and Teddy and our friend and hero Harry Nolan who we all thought would be president one day and who was going in the Army. And Sascha, who was Harry's bride, and my first, secret love, and Bloch's. We all loved Sascha. We went to the Blue Hill fair and from the fair we went and got drunk, all but Bloch who became the designated driver, and then there was fog on the road and he thought he saw a deer and swerved and that was when Sascha died.

It was enough for Bloch to think of the fair to think of all the rest of it now. It terrified him.

Nor had he ever felt human after that. That's what it came down to, or that's what he was feeling now, or that's what he was telling himself now. Why should he get a chance with Maisie's girls, why should they drive with him in a car, why should he impose on them his guilt, his fault, or his evil luck if that's all it was? He would have to protect them from himself. As always, he would have to make plans, take extra care, not put them in a situation. His courtesy was his shield. It stood between him and the disaster of those he loved. Lying in bed beside Maisie, Bloch felt a cool breeze come in on the tide and he cringed. The next day he said to Maisie there should be a change of plans. He would drive her to the airport and Bill Mason would follow them up and, after dropping Maisie, Bloch would leave the car at the Mercedes place and Bill Mason would drive him home.

"But how will you get to the fair?" Maisie asked. "I thought that was the whole idea."

"Maybe the car will be ready tomorrow. If not, Bill can drive us."

"But what if you need a car tonight?"

"I'll make sure that Bill's on call."

"Can't you rent a car?"

"It'll be easier just with Bill."

To Maisie it sounded contorted and more complicated than it needed to be, but it also sounded like Adam's care.

"The car really has to go in now?" she asked.

"It would be better if it went in when I was still around," he said. "Really, I didn't think of the brakes until last night."

He sounded so certain of it that she didn't question it further.

That night Bloch read to the girls from another of the McCloskey books that were all set near Clement's Cove. Then Maisie called and Alexandra and Margaret each got on a phone and the three of them talked as if the girls were off on the adventure of their lives. They both referred to Adam as "Daddy," which was as true and as normal as it could be, but still pleased him to hear, "Daddy" in the third person. He who'd been afraid he might never have a child. The girls slept in the rooms down the hall from his, each in her own bed. Maisie had wanted them to have their own rooms, had spent much of the summer getting the rooms finished.

In the morning Bloch called the Mercedes place in Bangor. They had found nothing wrong with the brakes but Bloch told them to keep the car and winterize it and go over it all. He told them he didn't need it right away. He'd have it picked up after he was gone. Bill Mason drove them to the fair, which was at first disappointing to Bloch, because it turned out to be a hippie fair, more that way than the Blue Hill Fair, anyway, and there was no cotton candy. But there were pigs and cows and sheep and guys on stilts with big noses and flashy pants, and the girls were happy. They even liked the soy dogs.

Maisie had Joni come over to make them dinner and make sure the girls were all packed up. Maisie had done most of the packing before she left but there were still toothbrushes and the clothes of the last couple days. Maisie surprised herself with these bursts of organization. She had never been organized before. She had been the crazy one, who didn't quite care. But now she cared about every detail. She talked to the girls another long time. She told them she'd see them tomorrow afternoon, she'd be at the airport, and was there anything special they wanted for dinner. Soy dogs, Margaret said.

Joni left and Bloch read to the girls again, the rest of the book from the night before, about girls who were going home after a long summer on an island. Then he put each to bed and kissed their foreheads and packed his own things to leave and thought of how wise he'd been to leave the car at the Mercedes place, it was better all around, and went to sleep.

CHAPTER 24

THERE WAS A RATTY COT AND A GAS HEATER in the garage where Freddy kept his limo and Freddy let Roy stay there. Having given up his place in Sedgwick, and being between employments, Roy had no other place. Freddy chided him about how a single male should not be quick to give up his own place, a lesson Freddy had learned on one occasion or another. Of course it was different once you were hitched, as was the case with himself and Marilyn, in that case there was no real alternative. But a single male had to look out for himself these days. The women had the power. The women made the rules. Freddy would have let Roy sleep in the limo itself, which would have been more comfortable than the ratty cot, but he was concerned that air freshener might not entirely remove the resultant smell. In a business that catered to the well-off, you had to attend to all the details.

It wasn't correct to say that Roy missed Verna. It was more correct to say how much worse his life was now, even after you subtracted out what a pain in the ass she had been. For this worsening of his circumstances, Roy came to blame Bloch more than he blamed Verna. He could see Verna's point of view. He could see how she'd think he was a screw-up. But what had brought her to that conclusion? Mainly, if you could put it in a category, it was Roy's interactions with this Mr. Bloch. Roy felt he had not been a hothead in quitting. The man was arrogant when all was said and done, he didn't know the depths of his own ignorance, and how do you work for someone like that, and anyway it was a dead-end situation. Roy continued to feel his life was worth more than dead-end situations.

And as further proof of all of it was Mr. Bloch's refusal to negotiate in any way, shape or manner concerning Verna's property, when Roy was flexible as hell, when he was even offering the man a bargain. There was something fishy there that Roy had never figured out. It was as if the man had some secret reason, so that he didn't act the way a normal rich guy would when offered what amounted to a steal. And Verna'd bought into all that, hook, line, and sinker. How she'd talk about him! What a decent fella he seemed to be! What nice neighbors to have! It just showed about rich people, no different from anybody else! It was almost like she wound up liking the guy more than she liked Roy.

It even got to the point, a couple of times, in Roy's thinking, where he imagined it wasn't beyond the realm of possibility that this Mr. Bloch had had his way with Verna. You never knew with these shy-looking guys. A lot of times that was exactly how they snuck in there, with that shy kind of look. And, too, there was Mrs. Bloch's tendency to be away with those kids quite a lot. Of course the one part of it that didn't make sense was the established fact this Mr. Bloch had owned a whole TV company, and if he wanted to spread his seed around there must have been some real beauties out there. Verna was nothing to look at. Even Roy had to admit to himself, that part put a hole in his theory.

One night Freddy and Marilyn had one of their once-every-other-week fights and Freddy came looking to find Roy for a bit of company. Roy had been spending more evenings than not at a tavern in Bar Harbor and they went over there together. In the course of commiserating and getting plastered, Freddy allowed how this last brawl might finally be the one that finished it for him and Marilyn. *Que sera, sera*, Freddy said, and then sang the translation off-key, while looking around the room to see if any women had walked in. It was a night of slim pickings, just like most of the others. The Bruins were playing on the television. Freddy said it would be a damn different story with Marilyn if he could have closed that deal for the limos. She was a woman who respected success. That's what it came down to. As he himself respected it. That's where they were alike.

Roy was feeling grateful toward Freddy and a little hopeful they might soon be in the same boat and he commiserated along. "These women don't have any faith," he said. "With them it's all got to be black-and-white, it's all got to be a done deal. Absolutely. You're absolutely right."

"Now you know I'm not one to criticize," Freddy said, "but you gave up with that New York fucker a little quick."

"You're referring to . . ."

"The New Yorker guy, the guy."

"Mr. Bloch?"

"The hell is this 'mister' shit?"

"You're right. No, you're right. I don't know why I say that. It's like copying Verna everything she says."

"You gave up on him a little too quick."

"You think I shouldn't of quit that job?"

"Hell, no. Quit. Absolutely right you quit. You weren't gonna go anywhere with that, getting paid by the hour to cut the guy's toenails. No, I'm talking about getting the man to buy her out. You'd've gotten that done, we'd be sitting pretty now. Both of us. Plus Verna. That's the point she didn't understand, correct? She didn't understand it would be *plus* Verna. She'd be among the first to benefit. And believe me, there's still plenty of opportunity."

"How so?"

"My friend, lest you forget, I'm still in business over here."

"Royce's daughter didn't sell his cars yet?"

"No, she sold his cars. She sold 'em, alright. To someone in *New Jersey*. You know what that means, don't you? Less competition around here. Less fleet chasing more business."

"So you're still looking to expand?"

"Absolutely. That Alice Gilmore didn't have the corner on previously owned limos. There's plenty around. You look online, they're all over."

"Well, if I could come up with the money, could I still be a part of the business?"

"The seat's still open at the table, partner."

It was the charm of that last word that warmed Roy up. If Freddy could still talk that way, could use the word "partner" and it didn't even sound sarcastic, then the last days and weeks of trouble might not all be a loss.

"'Course I don't have a clue where I could get that kind of money," Roy said.

"I know exactly where you could've. And you could still do it," Freddy said.

"You think? Cause the way I look at it, I'm fucked."

"Hell no. Your only problem, you gave up too quick. You didn't give the man enough hints."

"Hints. What hints?"

"Hints. Hints. Encouragements."

"I *gave* him hints. What about the garbage?"

"The garbage, yes. You put out garbage. Why should he give a fuck? He thinks you're a punk."

"Verna didn't want any more of that anyways."

"Verna's not part of it now, is she? Is Verna sitting here with us? Absolutely not."

"I thought of coyote piss once." Roy smiled easily in remembering it. "Put coyote piss on his porch."

"Oh that would be real effective. That would be tremendously effective."

"You know you can be a sarcastic fuck, Freddy."

"Listen to me." Freddy lowered his voice, almost like they were in a movie, almost like he really thought the barkeep, who was about halfway down the bar, would be listening. "Listen to me and shut up a second. The point is, not to get him to buy now. He's proved he's not gonna buy. So you got to get him to *sell*."

"Got it. Got it. You mean, because if he sold, then the next guy . . ."

"Whoever that is. Whoever that next guy is. Absolutely. You think the next guy's going to want that fucking trailer looking at his property? Anybody at all, anybody with a brain, once he's got that money invested, he's going to want Verna out of there. Which is good for all of us, right? Good for all of us, even her."

"Absolutely," Roy said. "Absolutely positively good for her." Roy tugged at his beer. "But just say, just say it was you who decided, what would *you* do, Freddy, to get him to sell?"

"What would I do? It's pretty obvious, isn't it? You don't do half measures. You don't act like a punk. First of all, you wait till he's gone, you wait till he's closed up for the season . . ."

"But he is gone."

"You told me he stayed on late."

"Yeah, but I happened to be by there. You know, just kind of checking . . ."

"On Verna? You are a pathetic individual."

"But his car's gone. Their car's gone."

"Oh, that's really *great*. The car's gone. What if they're out to a movie, fuckbrain?"

"Actually, okay. You want to know? I actually saw . . . I spoke to her."

"Verna?"

"And she told me the Blochs were gone. She saw them driving to the airport."

"Then, uh, the fuck are we waiting for?"

"Waiting for what?"

"There's only one thing ever got a man to think in a concentrated fashion about selling out. Lightning strikes his place. On a night when there's no lightning."

The number of beers they'd had, their desperation for any sort of success. These things put a hazy cloud of assent over what otherwise might have seemed a shaky proposition. As well, Roy sort of worshipped Freddy. Probably that was also a part of it. He aspired to be Freddy's partner in something.

As a result they never asked themselves, for instance, if Verna who would be the immediate beneficiary of all their plans would ever let Roy back into her life so that Roy and Freddy could benefit too. Nor did they reflect on the fact that Freddy knew little about arson, other than that his brother had burned down somebody's boathouse when he was seventeen and gotten caught for it. Nor did they think about where suspicion might fall if Bloch's house burned down. Or actually, the last they thought about a little bit. Freddy assured Roy that in cases like this the sheriff assumed it was an accident, because summer houses were always burning down, and a lot of times it was an insurance scam, but everybody looked the other way because they didn't want to get into legal hassles with rich people from away, and anyway the insurance premiums were too high, so there was some basic sympathy with the individual right there to start with. Roy did manage to ask, if everybody would believe it was an accident or an insurance scam, what there would be to persuade Mr. Bloch to sell out. But Freddy was thinking just then of the money that would be coming circuitously his way, and he forgot to answer and Roy forgot to ask again. It was a midnight adventure. It felt like taking back their world.

Freddy kept five gallon cans of gasoline in the garage where Roy was staying. They went back to get two of those first, and more beer and little bottles of vodka out of the minibar in the limo. They almost drove over in the limo itself, but Roy felt it might call too much attention to themselves, whereas if they took Roy's truck, just in case anybody saw them in Clement's Cove after midnight, it would seem only natural. Neither of them really questioned that reasoning either. A moonlit night and no one on the roads. From Bar Harbor to Clement's Cove, a distance of fifty miles, they passed only seven cars.

When they got to Bloch's road they parked at the bottom of it, so that the truck motor would not wake up Verna. They trudged up the road with the cans of gasoline and a few rags and such. They had continued to drink in the truck and that had quelled Roy's few doubts, that were anyway more like wispy contrails of his soul than anything that would really have stopped him. There was no car in the driveway of Bloch's house. Roy peered through the window panes of the garage to make sure there was none there either. The house was so dark that the moonlight shone brightly on it. Even Freddy could see that it was a damn pretty house and that all kinds of money had gone into it. A shame, in a way, but what could you do? Business was business. Something like that. No one else around. No one around at all, or so it seemed. A quiet lapping of the waves below them. Roy followed Freddy around, carrying the second can, while Freddy spilled gasoline here, there, and elsewhere. When he lit it there was no explosion, but quickly a ring of flame around the house. Roy and Freddy ran back down the road. They felt like freedom fighters. Fighting for their own freedom, anyway. They were gone quickly. Once they were out of Clement's Cove, they turned the radio up loud.

CHAPTER 25

THE FIRST THING BLOCH DID WHEN HE HEARD the smoke alarms screeching was grab for his bathrobe and put it on. He didn't want the girls to see him in his underpants. It was a silk robe he'd bought in Beverly Hills, one of the few things he ever bought for himself until he began to court Maisie, and he kept it on a chair by his bed as if you never knew what might happen suddenly in life. An old earthquake habit from California, perhaps. But when he awoke from a dream of whatever it was, he wasn't in California, he was on the coast of Maine and whatever might happen suddenly in life was happening then. Smoke poured up the stairs that he could see from his open door. He began to cough. He shouted the girls' names. He ran out into the hall.

Flames licked up under the smoke. They were consuming the carpet on the stairs and now the banisters caught fire. In bare feet Bloch ran around the fire, shouting the girls' names. More smoke alarms went off. They were screeching everywhere.

He ran into Margaret's room. She was sitting up in bed, crying for help, for Maisie. The flames were leaping outside her windows. Bloch lifted her up and kissed her forehead and ran with her through the connecting door to Alexandra's room.

Alexandra wasn't in her bed. Bloch put Margaret on Alexandra's bed and ran into her bathroom but she wasn't there either. He shouted her name. "Alexandra! Alexandra! Sascha!" It was the first time he'd ever called her Sascha. The smoke began to choke and blind him. He turned in the haze, this way and that. "Alexandra! Where are you? Sascha! Alexandra!"

He found her in the back of her closet, underneath her hanging party dresses, sitting on the floor with her knees up as if they alone would keep away the fire. He brought her back to where Margaret was. He got them to lie on the floor because the smoke was less there. He took one fraction of a second to thank God for Maisie who had put a phone in each of the girl's rooms because she spent so much time there and dialed the operator because Clement's Cove had no 9–1–1 and reported the fire. The operator was someplace a hundred miles away and had to look up wherever Clement's Cove was and then said she'd forward it right away.

Bloch would have waited then, because of the smoke and fire in the hall and out the windows, he would have waited for help and wet the blankets in the bathroom and lain close to the floor with the girls and wrapped the wet blankets around them all so they could breathe and put towels in the cracks of the doors, the way they were always instructing you in hotels in the event of fire. He was lucid then. His mind that had often thought clearly thought as clearly as it ever had. But then the fire burst open Alexandra's door and plaster fell and there was little left between them all and the flames that came in the door.

He herded the crying girls back through the connecting door. He grabbed the blankets from Margaret's bed and took them into Margaret's bathroom and soaked them in the tub and wrapped both the girls into both the blankets so they were like one big wet roll.

The fire in Alexandra's room burned through the connecting door into Margaret's. Bloch raced to the door opposite, which led back into the hall. He opened it to a curtain of fire. The knob was so hot it scorched his hand. He came back and grabbed up the big, wet roll that was Margaret and Alexandra. It didn't feel heavy, it felt almost light, and the cool touch of the soaking blankets was comforting. Still barefoot, in his silk bathrobe, with the bundle of the girls in his arms, Bloch felt, for once in his life, not exhilarated, but certain.

He walked as quickly as he could but didn't run, because he was afraid of dropping the girls. The flames were like all the accusers of his life. He would face them down, he would show them they weren't true, he would purify himself by being more than he had ever been. Or really, he couldn't help himself. He was lucid yet didn't know what he was doing. All he knew was that he was doing it. He was walking through the flames that were the accusers of his life as if they weren't even there. His rage would be greater than theirs. His rage, his sorrow, his revenge, would be greater. He would show them. Bloch who'd killed Maisie's sister. Bloch who didn't blink. Bloch with his guilt or fault or evil luck or whatever it was, who accused himself and took steps to protect the innocent of the world from himself. Bloch who'd once gotten lost in the fog and now it was as if that fog had turned suffocating and acrid and caught on fire. He would show them but show them what? Was Bloch not human, did he not bleed, did he not blink?

He walked through the hall, where the flames were huge, and down the stairs, where by now the flames were less. His feet were scorched. His robe caught fire. His hair caught fire. His flesh was burnt.

The one thing for certain he never thought was that this small, rather unprepossessing, older, wiry-haired man with a small pot belly and a wife he was lucky to have was doing anything like those things they were always doing in the movies. He had made such movies, or paid for them anyway. He had known guys who played such parts and they were different from himself.

He didn't even think he was redeeming his life. He would never have used those words.

And he didn't really know that he was afraid. He should have known, but he didn't. It was like something that in all the commotion got overlooked. The way Bloch's mother might once have put it, "in all the commotion."

Once down the stairs, he finally ran. In the thick darkness of the smoke, across the long entry hall of the house or what was left of it, dodging fallen charred beams, out the door, into air you could breathe, across the porch that was also burning, down the stone stairs, and into the night grass.

Verna, who had awakened to see the flames up the road, arrived to find the two girls in the grass, still wrapped together in their blankets like one of those sandwiches the Tradewinds made with the Lebanese bread, their faces smudged but their bodies unharmed. Scratches and bruises, seemed to be nothing more. They were whimpering softly. Margaret seemed on the verge of falling back asleep. Verna kissed them both, and untangled them a little from each other. Bloch was a little distance away, where he had rolled in the moist grass, in order to put the fire of his flesh out. He was still in his silk bathrobe, the charred shreds of it anyway. At points, at his shoulders in particular, the silk seemed to have fused with his flesh. He was unconscious. Verna gasped for how terrible he looked. The siren to call the volunteer firemen out of their beds began to wail.

III

CHAPTER 26

A CHAPTER ON ME AND BLOCH, MY ALTER EGO.

I had always confused myself with Adam Bloch. This went all the way back, to when I met him in college. Then he had been like the nerd, the flamer as we used to say. The maladroit one, the one who never had the right thing to say, the kid who couldn't blink, the Jew who gave Jews a bad name. And it further pissed me off that the friend whom I then very nearly worshiped, Harry Nolan, the guy we all thought would be president one day, was fond of Bloch as well.

Then Bloch was driving the car and I was in the backseat and Harry and his bride Sascha were in the front and Cord and Teddy Redmond were there too, and you already know the rest of that story.

The dark stain of Bloch. It's how I thought of it, never sure whether that dark stain was really myself.

We were the two outsiders, the two Jews, the two with our hidden ambitions, or whatever you would say.

Maybe I imagined that we looked too much alike, though we didn't really look much alike at all. I was taller, thinner, he had wiry hair. Bloch was always compact, just shy of pudgy, he looked like someone who would be hard to move if he didn't want to be. He had a stubborn look about him, always. Bloch looked a bit like my soul, perhaps, or what I imagined my soul to be, but not particularly like the guy who walked around and was called by my name.

Our lives crossed too many times. Yale. Harry. Sascha. When he was already rich, I brought him to California and helped him buy the company I worked for and he saved me my job. And there was Maisie too. My one-time lover. Bloch's bride. Clement's Cove. Bloch knew that I'd struggled to forgive him and maybe never had.

Not for Sascha's death, finally, but for the fact that he himself lived on. It was as if his very ability to survive anything seemed to make him what he was. Incapable of a broken heart?

Another thing, as the years passed, that I accused myself of. Being incapable of a broken heart. Or maybe it was simply that both our hearts, Bloch's and mine, had been broken so long ago and had never healed up. Hearts deep in waiting, watchful, injured, but alive. What is a heart if it's not that thing that's most deeply hidden? You could almost say that was a definition, find the most hidden thing and call it a heart. A definition for some of us, anyway.

Although, can you have a definition if it's not good for all? Bloch and I: he became the version of me I was most afraid to tell myself.

Then when he went and made all the money and saved me my job and was kind and started up with Maisie and came to Clement's Cove as if it were his project to become a human being at last, I came to see another version of me as him. For all those years of his ascendance it had been taking shape, but it crystallized, I think, at the wedding. Bloch playing his cello in the storm. Me if I'd gone all the way. Me if my own broken heart had been as large as his, if I'd suffered the same catastrophe.

I went off on my fellowship to Europe. Bloch stayed behind, in this place where we'd been thrown together in tragedy thirty-odd years before. I've of course had to imagine a lot of what he said or thought or exactly how he did things. But you see, I knew him well. Or I thought I did. I thought he was almost me. It turned out he wasn't. Not at all.

CHAPTER 27

SOMETHING ABOUT BLOCH AND MONEY.

He scored 800 on his math College Board, in the days before they inflated the scores. He could do columns of figures in his head, multiplications and long divisions in his head.

He liked to win. But he was not a sore loser. He simply resolved to win the next time.

His memory was good.

He was good at *Monopoly*.

He made his first fortune in stone-washed jeans and then a larger one in network TV and a still larger one in cable TV and then he was the only one of the Hollywood guys, or the only one I heard of, anyway, to see the potential of the Internet early. The rest of them just sat there and choked on the envy of it all when the kids up north made their piles. And then sometime early in 1999 Bloch sold out of the Internet too. None of us knew at the time that this was a smart thing to do. We thought only that he'd fallen for Maisie and didn't care about the rest any-more. Later he was fond of quoting Bernard Baruch, who apparently told people the secret of his fortune was that he sold too soon. Bloch must have thought he was a little like Bernard Baruch then. He must have read a book about him.

It was something he could do, make money, when there were so many simpler things that he couldn't do. He would wonder sometimes why people marveled at his gift, or knack, or developed skill, or whatever it was. He never valued it especially highly. But he knew it was what he had to work with. He was not blind to what money could do.

He was generous with his money. Not flashy, but generous and orderly and even slyly sweet. Not one to put his name on hospital wards or museum wings, to want to know where the name would go before he wrote the check. He simply wrote the check. Bloch was not a scholar, but somewhere he had heard of a Talmudic teaching that the highest acts of charity were those done in secret.

Once a year he counted his money, or estimated it anyway, ballparked it on a piece of paper. But the year he married Maisie, he forgot.

And then there were the times when he hated it.

Because it wore him like a suit rather than the other way around.

Because it wouldn't go away when he told it to.

Because he couldn't even hate it without feeling ungrateful.

Because it had a way of insinuating that it was all that he was.

But his hating it was only a low-grade fever, really. Mostly he got along. Mostly he played the cards that he was dealt.

CHAPTER 28

SOMETHING ABOUT VERNA'S FAMILY.

Clement's Cove from its earliest days had been a good safe harbor to go fishing from. The founding family were the Clements, or as some have had it, the Clementses, who came down the coast from the vicinity of York sometime after the Revolution. Soon after them came the Masons and the Hubbards. Edward Hubbard moved his family from Newburyport, Massachusetts for the promise of cheap land and a fresh start in what was then a forested and isolated place.

By then the Indians were gone. The wars with the French had all but eliminated them from the coast.

Edward and his sons and grandsons fished for mackerel and cod. They didn't have to go far to find them. They fished "on shares," which meant that the catch of the whole boat was divided equally among all the fishermen aboard. No one was labor, no one was boss.

In the Civil War, five Hubbards fought. Horace Hubbard, age twenty-two, was killed at Gettysburg. William Hubbard, age twenty, died of typhus in a Confederate prison.

After the war, the canning plants came to the coast. John Hubbard and Clarence Hubbard and the first Everett Hubbard fished for herring that went to the plants and came out as sardines.

For twelve years or so there were weirs on Clement's Cove, so that the fish were caught right there.

A couple of the women in the family, Sarah Hubbard and Dorothy Morris, became schoolteachers. The others stayed close to Clement's Cove, or went over to Deer Isle or Sedgwick, and raised their families. The Hubbards became intermarried with the Morrises, the Audrys, the Cumminses, the Earlys, the Hutchinsons, and a few others, but never with the Clements. The two families didn't get on. It may have been they were too close neighbors.

The Masons and the Clements sold their land off to rusticators starting around 1880, and the Hubbards sold some off, too, since it wasn't worth a damn for farming, but John Hubbard was the first of the Hubbards to hesitate about doing so. He didn't believe in selling land off.

Summer houses were built, around but not on, the Hubbards' land.

Frederick Hubbard, age twenty-four, died when the

USS Maine exploded. He was one of six Mainers killed aboard that ship.

John Hubbard Junior went out to Alaska to seek his fortune in the gold fields, and there were those who said he found one there. But he never came back. No one knew for sure what happened to him.

James Hubbard, age twenty, died in the Argonne forest. Another Edward Hubbard, age eighteen, died at the Second Battle of the Marne.

In 1923, Franklin Hubbard put a motor on his boat for the first time. By then the fish were farther from shore than they had been. In that same year, 1923, the Elliot family from Tennessee built their first shingle cottage on the cove.

In 1926, Millicent Hubbard, Franklin's second daughter, won a scholarship to go to Bates College in Lewiston.

During the Depression, Franklin Hubbard sold off more of the family land than he would have liked to do.

Daniel Hubbard, age twenty, died in the Battle of Monte Cassino.

By the nineteen seventies, the fish were nearly gone. William Hubbard and his son Everett Hubbard turned to lobstering, and a certain Hubbard whose name was not often mentioned, to protect the innocent, was said to have turned to marijuana smuggling.

In 1971, Janice Hubbard, a first cousin of Verna's, age twenty-four, died when the C-130 she was flying in crashed on a supply mission en route to TanSonNhat Airport, Republic of Vietnam.

In 1994, Everett Hubbard died, and Verna was left the last Hubbard living on Clement's Cove.

CHAPTER 29

SOMETHING ABOUT BLOCH AND JUSTICE.

I read this once, I'm not even sure it's true: that the measure of a just man is not how he yearns for justice when he is oppressed, but whether he still yearns for it when he is no longer oppressed.

CHAPTER 30

A DREAM OF ROY'S.

She tells him to get in the pool with her.

He tells her, "It's too damn hot, you get in your own damn pool," which is just teasing, because he gets in with her.

It's like Verna's lost twenty pounds, he's about to tell her, "You lost twenty pounds," when it's not Verna at all, it's Maisie, she said to call her Maisie, so he says, "You lost twenty years."

And she says, "Thank you very much. I feel like I did."

In the pool they get so close they're rubbing against each other and for sure, he thinks, this'll cost him his job, but instead she says, "This'll cost Mr. Bloch his job."

Roy grabs her breasts then and she grabs him and they go at it for several seconds till all the water's drained out of the pool.

CHAPTER 31

A LETTER WAS WAITING FOR ME AT THE POST office. It had been there more than two weeks and Arnie Simmons, who was postmaster, was beginning to wonder what to do with it. He would have returned it to sender, he said, but the sender was someplace in Shanghai, China and he wasn't sure what the postal authorities in China did with letters stamped "return to sender." One of those dilemmas you faced in mail delivery, damned if you do and damned if you didn't. Arnie was glad to see me. What had it been? A year and a half? The way it worked, you only get one year of forwarding. So that, too, had made him uncertain what to do. Can't just turn off the hearing aid to regulations entirely.

The letter was from Maisie. It was on hotel stationery. One of the chains, Four Seasons, I think. I read it in the post office parking lot, halfway to my rental car, on that bone-damp afternoon of my arrival back in Clement's Cove. It began:

> *Old friend. I'm not sure how much of this you know. Or, of course, if you'll even receive this. But I thought I ought to try. You know you could cease being a jerk about it and get e-mail by now. Have you, maybe? Let me know if you have. Though I'm not sure I would wish to put this in an e-mail.*
>
> *Adam is dead. I suppose that's the first thing I should say. He died on October 29, 2000, in Jerusalem, Israel. How he got there, why he got there, I'm not even sure I can say.*

She then related to me the facts of the matter regarding Bloch's staying on with the girls when she went back to New York, and the fire, and the fact it was arson, and what Adam did to save the girls. Pretty much as I've written them.

The letter went on:

> *It was almost a miracle he survived at all. It's what the doctors said. Third-degree burns, seventy percent of his body. The trauma, the chances of infection. They flew him to Boston, to Mass General. They sedated him, kept him unconscious. I came up. It was this almost unbelievably schizophrenic experience, because I was so relieved about the girls, and so hor-*

rified about him. I almost couldn't balance it. They wouldn't even let me get close to him. He was in one of these tents. The infection danger. Also, they had to cool his body. It was so burnt, any heat alone could have killed him. If I'm perfectly, totally honest, I suppose there was something merciful in my being unable even to see him well then. I'm afraid I would have averted my eyes. And if I had, I would never have forgiven myself. Never, not ever. Yet I wanted to kiss him. Kiss his lips, I think. Be balm for his lips.

But I think his lips . . . what's the point of even saying?

I returned to the city. There was a plan to bring him by air ambulance to New York Hospital. I approved it. I thought it was a good idea. Then the day before we were going to move him, I got word that he'd regained consciousness. They'd lessened the sedation. I was going to fly up right away. But they said don't, he's still in his tent, by the time I got there he'd probably be asleep again. It was only one night. I said okay.

The next day he didn't show up. I was at the hospital waiting. We called Newark Airport. We called the air ambulance company. They said I'd have to speak to one of the directors. I was going crazy. I thought he must have died en route. You know the way, if a plane crashes, they put on the board, "see agent."

But it wasn't that. I was told there'd been a change of itinerary, at the patient's express request. I said well could they possibly explain to me the wife what the fucking change of itinerary was? They said they couldn't because it was a matter of patient confidentiality. I said fine but I was the goddamn wife and my husband's life was in danger and if they didn't tell me I'd sue their ass into the Hudson River by sunset. They said they were sorry but it was a question of confidentiality, at the express request of the patient.

I went ballistic. I know, it sounds like I'd already gone ballistic, but then I went really ballistic. I screamed and threatened and probably called up everything I'd ever learned at McLean's about going crazy, and finally the guy said he could understand my distress but he would have to get back to me and he hung up. So I did, I called up Debevoise and we sued them the next day. Sued Mass General, too, when they weren't cooperative either. They said they knew nothing about it, it wasn't their business, the patient was released. Finally, one of the doctors, who we also sued, said, just as a matter of rumor, something he'd heard indirectly, so he didn't think it would be violating doctor–

patient privilege, but something about going to Israel.

I called up every hospital in Israel that had a trauma center in it. And it was unbelievable, but I found him. He was in Hadassah Hospital, Jerusalem, registered under his own name. It was a place that had an international reputation for trauma, and it allowed me for a few seconds to imagine he'd chosen it for its excellence of care, that's why he'd snuck away from us all, he was going for the excellent treatment and as soon as he was better he would come back. But it wasn't that, of course. Whatever it was, it wasn't that. Among other things, you can't get much more excellent than Mass General or New York Hospital. I flew out that night. I wanted to surprise him. Or I imagined all sorts of things, him refusing to see me, him engineering another escape. But by the time I got there, he was gone. He'd died early in the morning. The doctors' fear of an overwhelming infection had been realized.

I've spent more time than I could ever admit wondering what made him run away, and in such a perilous, awful condition. You know the facts now as I know them, so, dear Louie, you may have as good a guess as mine. Maybe better. Maybe I'm too close to it. But what I imagine, what I think . . . pretty basic, I guess, pretty dumb of me . . . but I imagine he felt guilty. About me, about all of it.

And asking himself all those "if's," replaying the trauma of Sascha. I imagine he didn't feel like a hero at all. I imagine he thought that single, selfless act of his was normal, the least you could expect of a person. Or no, not a person. A person who'd screwed so much up. A person who was never out of debt, no matter how much money he had. I imagine—and this is the worst part of it for me—that he even felt guilty for being the one who said he'd like the girls to stay so he could take them to the fair.

So maybe he ran away because he couldn't face us? Felt he didn't deserve us?

Embarrassment, the silent killer. Do you think so, Louie? Please. I'm not telling you. I'm asking you. He was my husband and I feel I knew nothing. Worse, that I didn't try hard enough to know, when he was alive.

And going to Israel. Why Israel? All the time I'd known him, he'd never made anything of being Jewish. Not to me, anyway. But then, maybe he wouldn't. What about to you? Did he ever to you? Tell me if I'm wrong. But then I thought, Israel's supposed to be that place where a Jew can go when nobody else wants him.

I even imagined he'd made arrangements, if he died to be buried on Mount Scopus, or wherever that cemetery is, I'm not sure I've got this right, but I've read it, a lot of Jews, from all over the world, they decide they want to be buried there. Talk about feeling like an outsider. Me trying to have a coherent thought about that. Me trying to imagine a place where you can go when nobody else wants you.

My life's been too lucky. I've had this shitty disease, but my life's been too lucky.

But he hadn't made any such arrangements. Or at least the hospital wasn't aware of them. They gave me his remains and I felt like one of those Army guys who has to bring the bodies home. His parents were gone. There was no one to consult. I had him cremated, then spent weeks thinking about what to do with the ashes. Selfish, probably, nothing but selfish, but over Christmas, on Mount Desert, you know some piece of our family always goes up there for Christmas, I put the ashes in the family plot. By Sascha's grave, and Harry's, and where maybe mine will be one day. The ground wasn't quite frozen, but it was still a hell of a job. I loved digging that hole. One thing I could do, dig that hole.

So there. End of story? I doubt it. I don't know what I'll be feeling about any of it a year from now. I myself am well, by the way. Physically, I mean.

Clear on all the latest batch of tests. The girls, also well. They miss Adam. They don't understand. They really were charmed by him, finally. They loved that fair he took them to.

Probably you've heard this, if you've heard anything at all, but the state police caught two men for the crime. One was very briefly our caretaker, maybe you know him, Roy Soames, who lived with that woman in the trailer for awhile. I always thought he was cute. Isn't that terrible? Adam thought he was trouble from the start. I can't even think about that part.

Or yes, I can. I was unkind to Adam. I was unfair to him. I didn't see him, for God's sake.

Roy and his friend, a guy from Mount Desert, are charged with murder. The truth is, I feel horrid for them too. They didn't mean murder.

But beyond that. There are nights, like the nights Adam must have lived, when I'm certain it was all my fault, I started it all, like the Helen of Clement's Cove. It's just how it was.

I've brought the girls here, to Shanghai, so that they could be in a place where most of the faces look more like theirs. Probably not necessary, but anyway, we're here. Shanghai, as you've probably read, is exploding. We've been living in a hotel up to now, which means the girls have been getting to live like little Eloises. I've made a few friends. The kids go to a bilingual school and are starting to learn Chinese. I've even talked to people about starting the kind of breakfast joint I had in Taos. There are plenty of ex-pats who would likely appreciate it. But most probably we'll come home after not too long.

About Adam Bloch. My husband. My friend. My lover, too. You know, we were *lovers, sometimes it didn't seem like it, but we were. The one thing that keeps me sleepless and brings tears to my eyes is my fear that he died feeling unloved. Please, Louie, tell me if you can, that it was otherwise. But I don't think you can.*

Maisie

IV

CHAPTER 32

IN THE GENERAL STORE THERE WAS A DIFference of opinion as to what some said was a key piece of evidence. Lewis Early maintained that the fact Roy checked out the garage before they set the fire showed an intent to do no bodily harm. Tom Benson, who was more Roy's pal than some of the others, concurred that it meant Roy was not too bad a fella, really, kind of a weak sister was all it was, he just got his head turned around by a set of bad circumstances and unfortunate company from over to Bar Harbor, but it wasn't his nature to injure or kill. Tom added that it would be just like Roy, to look in that garage first and make sure it was empty. On the other side of the argument was chiefly Burt Cummins, whose main point was that felony murder was felony murder. According to Burt, you didn't have to intend to kill or even maim, all you had to do was intend to commit a certain felony, in this case arson, and if a death resulted, that was it, you were guilty of felony murder. Mac, Bonnie, and a few others deferred to Burt's apparent expertise on this subject. But Tom Benson said, all well and good, but that didn't mean it was right, to convict a man of murder in these circumstances. Go take it up with the geniuses in Augusta, Burt Cummins said. You could usually score a few points in the general store by referring anything back to the geniuses in Augusta. Another point of discussion was whether Mr. Bloch's death could properly be attributable to anything Roy did, including the arson. The point here, Lew Early said, was that nobody really knew the suspicious circumstances in which Mr. Bloch died. If it was okay for him to fly all the way over to Jerusalem, Israel, he couldn't've been in too bad health, could he now? Lew admitted he didn't know as much law as Burt Cummins, but for instance if those doctors over there messed something up and that's why he died, then you couldn't pin that back on old Roy, could you? And that whole thing about going over there, said Tunk Smith, to Israel when you're sick like that, what was that all about? Mr. Bloch ought to take some responsibility here, Roy oughtn't to bear all of it, Tunk said.

Although, according to Ralph Audry, Verna felt he should. Verna, according to Ralph, felt that Roy deserved whatever he got, which according to rumor and the best estimates anybody could come up with, would probably be about seven years in the penitentiary. Tom Benson said you had to take in account Verna's position here.

Of course she wasn't going to go light on Roy, he said, it didn't make sense, after all he'd put her through.

But Ralph said her feelings had more to do with the fact it was evil what was done to Mr. Bloch. That was the strong word she was using, the evil done to him, Ralph said. According to Verna, it wasn't every man, no matter what they would say when they weren't personally involved, who would have got himself all burned up to the point of dying to save two little girls. Some would, sure, but a lot wouldn't. A lot would go only halfway, or get burned only a little and that would be it. Bonnie said she'd heard Verna express opinions similar to these. Verna felt Mr. Bloch was a very decent man, according to Bonnie.

Everyone could agree with that, Mac said, nobody was disputing that part, Mr. Bloch was a great performer in that fire. And Roy was a numbnuts for sure. But the whole thing was a tragedy. That's all you could really say about it.

I was there for that discussion. I asked how Verna was doing. Bonnie said she was doing pretty good, she took a couple weeks off to go see her sister in Vermont, but she was back now and cleaning houses. Then I told the others I'd received a letter from Bloch's widow and that she and her little girls were in Shanghai, China. Tunk Smith wanted to know what she was doing there and I said I didn't really know for sure. Was it for one of those eastern medical treatments, Carl Henry asked, and I said no, she was well now. And I added that I imagined she just wanted to be away. Then Con Stephens asked me if I happened to know how much she was wanting for that property of hers. I said I didn't know that, either. Then Mac asked me how well I really knew this Mr. Bloch. I said I knew him a long time.

CHAPTER 33

THAT SUMMER THE WRECKERS AND BULLDOZers came and they tore down what was left of Bloch's Folly. A lot of salvage, a lot of Italian flagstone, they said. Even the foundations were dug out, so that the new owners, Goldman Sachs people from New Canaan, Connecticut, could start over. They had a different idea for their house on the coast. More windows, more light. Making the most of the view. A house more like the Hamptons, unafraid of glass and steel. And Maisie's lap pool was not enough for them. They wanted a spa and an invisible edge and black tiles and a waterfall, everything the previous owners had disdained. It was all going to cost a fortune.

Verna watched the same workmen come and go. The new owners' attorneys called and made her offers. She was still not selling.

ABOUT THE AUTHOR

Jeffrey Lewis won two Emmys and many other honors as a writer and producer of *Hill Street Blues*. His "Meritocracy Quartet" charts the progress of a generation from the '60s through the '90s. The first book of the quartet, *Meritocracy: A Love Story*, won both the Independent Publishers Book Award for General Fiction and the *ForeWord* Book of the Year Silver Award for Fiction. *Meritocracy* (1960s) is followed by *The Conference of The Birds* (1970s), *Theme Song for an Old Show* (1980s), and now *Adam the King* (1990s). All titles are available from Other Press. Jeffrey Lewis lives in Los Angeles and Castine, Maine.

Lewis, Jeffrey.
Adam the king

4/16/21	DATE DUE		